"Jenny, EVERY TIME I'M AROUND YOU, MY GAME plan goes right out the window," Carter said, moving closer to her.

She looked quizzical. "Game plan?"

He shrugged, with a husky laugh that made her yearn to hear it again. "Before I walked in the door, my thoughts were organized. I knew what I wanted to discuss with you and how long it would take. But being around you disrupts my thoughts, punches holes in my logic, and trashes any plan I come up with."

She couldn't help feeling mildly annoyed that he'd come to see her with a plan and a timetable. "Maybe you need to loosen up, Carter. Life doesn't always go according to plan. Some things are just beyond our control," she suggested softly.

"That's true," he said. "I didn't plan to let you get under my skin." His smile was slow and devastatingly sensual. "But you do get to me, Jenny. You do. . . ."

WHAT ARE *LOVESWEPT* ROMANCES?

They are stories of true romance and touching emotion. We believe those two very important ingredients are constants in our highly sensual and very believable stories in the LOVE-SWEPT line. Our goal is to give you, the reader, stories of consistently high quality that may sometimes make you laugh, sometimes make you cry, but are always fresh and creative and contain many delightful surprises within their pages.

Most romance fans read an enormous number of books. Those they truly love, they keep. Others may be traded with friends and soon forgotten. We hope that each LOVESWEPT romance will be a treasure—a "keeper." We will always try to publish

LOVE STORIES YOU'LL NEVER FORGET
BY AUTHORS YOU'LL ALWAYS REMEMBER

The Editors

PERFECT TIMING

THERESA GLADDEN

BANTAM BOOKS
NEW YORK · TORONTO · LONDON · SYDNEY · AUCKLAND

PERFECT TIMING

A Bantam Book / August 1994

*If you would be interested in receiving protective vinyl covers for your
Loveswept books, please write to this address for information:*

Loveswept
Bantam Books
P.O. Box 985
Hicksville, NY 11802

ISBN 0-553-44344-5

Published simultaneously in the United States and Canada

Bantam Books are published by Bantam Books, a division of Bantam Dou-
bleday Dell Publishing Group, Inc. Its trademark, consisting of the words
"Bantam Books" and the portrayal of a rooster, is Registered in U.S.
Patent and Trademark Office and in other countries. Marca Registrada.
Bantam Books, 1540 Broadway, New York, New York 10036.

PRINTED IN THE UNITED STATES OF AMERICA

OPM   0 9 8 7 6 5 4 3 2 1

This book is for family and good friends—
Elaine Rosamond Hays
Jennifer Laura Gladden
Lisa Cantrell
Yvonne Trom
Lynn Brisson
Rena Vaughn
—with love and gratitude.

PROLOGUE

He was perfect for her baby sister.

Maureen Robbins smiled across her desk at the man. Although his chin almost rested on the knees of his sharply creased suit trousers, he didn't look at all uncomfortable or ill at ease sitting in one of the child-size chairs in her third grade classroom.

She gave him an *A+* for being a good sport.

He unfolded from the chair and stood up. "Thank you for your time, Mrs. Robbins. You've been very helpful. I'll contact Jenny Johnson today."

Another *A+* for politeness, for his appreciation of others' efforts, and for his determination to follow through.

"You're welcome." She came around her desk.

He smiled. She smiled back.

"I really think the Sunshine Girls Club will help Tiffany," she reaffirmed, walking to the door with him. "Jenny is the most compassionate person I know. You and Tiffany will like her."

"I hope so. Again, I appreciate your advice."

"My pleasure. Tiffany is a bright little girl. I'm happy to have her in my class. And try not to worry so much about her. She just needs time to adjust to the changes in her life and to realize you aren't going to abandon her."

Incredulity spread across his face. "Abandon her? You think my daughter is afraid I'll abandon her?"

Mmmm. Definitely a *C* for perceptiveness, Maureen thought. "Children sometimes experience the death of a parent as abandonment. It's a normal reaction."

He looked upset. "That never occurred to me. What can I do about it?"

She smiled, giving him extra credit for loving his daughter enough to swallow his masculine pride and ask for help. "Give her time. Just keep letting Tiffany know you love her and she'll be all right. Get her involved with the Sunshine Girls. Being with other kids who have experienced similar situations will also help." She patted his arm. "Try not to be too concerned about it."

He nodded, and she could see the wheels turning in his mind as he took to heart what she'd said. "Thank you again for everything, Mrs. Robbins."

"My pleasure. Let me know if there's anything I can do for Tiffany here at school."

"I will." He shook her hand.

Maureen watched him leave with her sister's phone number and address tucked in the inner pocket of his suit jacket. Then she grinned all the way back to her desk because she'd just bagged two birds with one terrific piece of advice. It pleased her no end that she was helping a sweet but troubled child and sending her sister a hunk of a man at the same time.

She sat down to grade papers. Should she tell Jenny what she'd done? No. Forewarned was forearmed, as the saying went.

She just hoped Jenny wouldn't brush this guy off too quickly or try to turn him into a friend, the way she had with all the other potential mates Maureen had introduced her to over the past three years.

If you dare blow this one off, Jen, I'll . . .

She'd what? Maureen thought as she stamped a grinning cat at the top of a student's paper. Keep trying, of course.

But darn it. Carter Dalton really was perfect for her baby sister.

ONE

"Hello. Don't bother me." The voice that answered the phone was sweet and childlike.

"May I speak with Jenny Johnson?" Carter ran a frustrated hand through his hair.

"Hello. Don't bother me," the voice repeated. There was an odd noise—it sounded like fingernails scraping and scratching on the telephone receiver—then the connection was broken.

Carter stared at the dead receiver for several moments. He'd called the Johnson woman's home every half hour since returning to his office at noon, and each time he'd spoken to that same child and had gotten that same strange response.

Swearing silently, he replaced the receiver. He swiveled around in his chair and gazed blindly out the window. It was a beautiful day outside, the first day in early April that Greensboro, North Carolina, hadn't been held hostage by cold, wet, wintery weather. He wasn't in any mood to appreciate it, though. His concentration was shot, his patience worn thin.

A man can't raise a little girl all by himself.

For eight months those words had lived in his mind, like an insidious phobia. They ambushed him at times, when he was worried about his daughter, undermining his confidence as a parent.

Negative thinking was a fearsome enemy, he thought as he rubbed the tight muscles in his neck. He couldn't afford to turn his back on that enemy for even a second. Tiffany was depending on him.

She had suffered so many broken relationships —the divorce of her parents, the death of her mother, being uprooted from family and friends. A quiet, shy child, she never vocalized her unhappiness or the loneliness and helplessness she must be feeling. Yet he could see its sad reflection in her big blue eyes. He could feel it in her stillness. He could hear it in her silence.

Somehow he had to make it right for her. He'd do anything to make her happy again. And if her teacher thought the Sunshine Girls Club would help his little Tiffy make friends and adjust, then he'd move heaven and earth to get her into the club.

But to do that he had to contact Jenny Johnson, the club's organizer and adult leader.

Turning to face his desk, he scowled at the phone. He made his living finding creative solutions to problems. Getting in touch with that

Johnson woman by phone was turning out to be a problem.

Carter glanced at his watch. Four-thirty. He didn't usually leave the office until six, not even on Fridays. He weighed the importance of the time and motion study project he was working on for his new client against his need to contact Jenny Johnson. The latter won out.

He got up and grabbed his jacket.

"Don't you just love Fridays, Mom!"

"TGIF." Jenny took her eyes off the road long enough to smile at her eight-year-old daughter.

She remembered how much she'd loved Fridays when she was Lara's age. Weekends might not hold the same kind of magic for her now, but the day still came wrapped in good feelings, feelings somehow softer, warmer, a bit like coming home after being away for a while.

Jenny negotiated a left turn and slowed the minivan to a crawl. They lived on a street where tall elms provided cool green shade, and in the summer served as pirate ships, castles, and anything else the neighborhood kids could imagine.

Jenny watched their three-bedroom house come into view. The frame dwelling was old and unimpressive compared to the huge contemporary house she and Greg used to live in. But this cozy little place was all hers. She loved it, cranky plumbing and all.

When she and Lara had moved into the house, it had been run-down and neglected. At first, fixing it up had given her something to think about besides her ex-husband and his sudden need to prove he hadn't lost his youthful virility along with most of his hair.

As her new home and yard had changed, taken on renewed life, she'd also changed and revitalized. By the time she'd applied the last coat of interior paint, she'd realized that her self-esteem had returned stronger than ever.

Nuts to you, Greg, she thought, mentally thumbing her nose at her ex-husband. He could have his candy-apple-red convertible and his college girls. She had a great kid, a home full of laughter and pets, and no one to get picky over a little dust on the furniture or a cobweb or two.

She parked in the single-car drive beside the house. Lara was already out of the van and doing a jig on the grass as Jenny got out.

"Mom, watch me."

Smiling at the center of her universe, Jenny watched her daughter drop her school book bag and dash across the lawn. Lara's long, coltish legs rose up in the air as she executed a back walkover.

"That's terrific."

Lara beamed a smile. "My teacher says I'll be ready for competition by summer."

"That's wonderful, sweetie."

"Come on, Mom. Swing me around. Please, please, please!"

Jenny instantly recalled the adorable three-year-old who used to hold out her chubby little arms and beg, "Swing me, Mama, swing me." Grinning, she tossed her canvas gym bag and purse on the bottom porch step, then walked over to her daughter.

They locked hands and spun slowly in a circle. A bit faster. Faster. Building the momentum. They twirled around and around until they both grew dizzy and fell to the ground, laughing and breathless.

Looking down at the small face that so closely resembled her own, Jenny smiled softly. Sometimes she missed the sweet baby Lara used to be, but she wouldn't turn back the clock, even if she could. Lara was happy, healthy, and well adjusted. That was the most important and rewarding part of Jenny's life.

Every day Jenny thanked God that her little girl wasn't traumatized by the divorce and that she was secure enough to bear her father's indifference.

"That was fun," Lara said. "Let's do it again."

"Maybe later." Jenny tugged gently on the long braid resting upon her daughter's shoulder. "Your old mother is hot and sweaty. And Happy needs to be let out. I bet he has all four legs crossed by now."

"Okay. Race you. Last one to the door is a rotten egg." Lara jumped up and ran toward the house.

Jenny took off after her, pausing just long enough to gather up their belongings. With Lara singing, "Na-na-na, you're a rotten egg," while hopping from one foot to the other, Jenny unlocked the door.

Happy was waiting for them in the foyer. The Saint Bernard barked and pranced around them.

"Braaak! Bad, bad, bad. Off with your head," squawked T-Beau from his perch on the banister. Grumbling in a language Jenny didn't understand, the parrot swooped over her head, then beat wings into the living room.

Fighting off Happy, who thought he was a cute little lap dog and was trying to jump into her arms, Jenny looked around to see why the bird was miffed. The living room seemed fine. T-Beau's cage was open, his birdseed dish was empty. She thought he was just hungry until she saw a movement in his cage.

"So that's it." She pushed the dog away and went to capture the gerbil trying to hide behind T-Beau's water dish.

The parrot dive-bombed the cage, his wings flapping so hard, she could hear them beat the air. "Braaak! Either you or your head must be off, off, off."

She handed the gerbil to Lara. "Return this little guy to his cage. Feed that cranky bird too."

"No pepper," T-Beau said. "Pepper makes people hot tempered." He perched on the dog's broad back. Accustomed to the parrot using him for transportation, Happy merely looked resigned.

Lara cuddled the gerbil against her chest. "Okay. Then can I go outside to practice my walk-overs?"

"May I," Jenny automatically corrected.

"You sound like Aunt Maureen." Lara rolled her eyes. "Mother, may I?"

"Yes, you may. Happy needs to go out, so take him with you. I'm going to take a shower."

As Lara took charge of the animals, Jenny headed upstairs. In her bedroom, she stretched her tired muscles. She'd put in five hours of work that morning at the church where she was employed part-time as a secretary, and an hour at the YMCA where she taught step aerobics while Lara took gymnastics, and she'd fended off Hank Flowers's customary Friday pass.

According to her sister, Hank was the undis-puted "blond Adonis" of the Nautilus set at the Y, and she thought Jenny was crazy for refusing to go out with him. But he just didn't turn her on, as the saying went in her youth.

Men had been marked off Jenny's personal list of necessities long ago. Especially self-involved men like Hank who were more handsome than she was pretty. She'd married one of those. It was a mistake she would never repeat.

Jenny took a pair of jeans and a shirt out of the closet. Her underwear drawer, though, was a dis-appointment. The only item in it was a black lace bra, an optimistic gift from her sister, one she'd never worn. It would have to do. Sweaty beggars who put off doing laundry couldn't afford to be choosy.

Now where were the panties that matched the bra? she wondered. She hadn't worn them either, so they had to be around somewhere.

Carter parked on the street in front of Jenny Johnson's house, then got out of his car and stood on the sidewalk for a moment.

She lived in an older neighborhood located near the University of North Carolina. Her home was a modest two-story, painted gray-blue with trim the color of a good burgundy wine. Jonquils and daffodils dotted the yard. Dogwood trees and azaleas loaded with red, pink, and white buds were ready to bloom any day now.

A tawny-haired girl dressed in tights and a leotard turned cartwheels on the recently mowed lawn. She didn't appear to be more than eight or nine. Mrs. Robbins had said Jenny Johnson was divorced and had a daughter who was a member of the Sunshine Girls Club.

A black-and-white Saint Bernard was sprawled on the porch. The moment Carter set foot on the lawn, the dog started barking its fool head off. It rushed down the steps, disturbing the black cat sleeping on the bottom one. The cat got in a good swipe at the dog's hind quarter, then leapt into the shrubbery.

"Happy! Come back here," the little girl yelled as the dog ran toward him.

Carter stood still, his muscles tensing in anticipation of an attack. Glancing around, he looked for something, a stick or anything, with which to defend himself.

The girl ran over and grabbed the dog by the collar. "Happy, sit."

Incredibly, the creature sank to its haunches. Its big pink tongue lolled out in a doggie grin.

The girl shook her finger in its hairy face. "Shake hands with the nice man and say you're sorry."

"The nice man" warily eyed the paw the Saint Bernard lifted. "Does he bite?" Carter asked.

"Oh, no. Happy would never be so rude. He didn't mean to scare you. He just wanted to play with you."

Carter wasn't convinced, but he gave the furry paw a quick shake anyway. "Do you live here?"

Big brown eyes skimmed over him, sizing him up in the open way kids did. Those eyes were thickly lashed and set in a cute pixie face. "Uh-huh. My name's Lara Johnson. I've seen you before."

"You have?" Carter looked down at the dog. It was chewing on his shoelace. He moved his foot out of the way.

She bobbed her head. "I saw you at my school.

You were with the new girl who's in my aunt Maureen's class."

"Mrs. Robbins is your aunt?" He wondered why Mrs. Robbins hadn't mentioned her relationship to the Johnsons.

"She's my mom's sister. Aunt Mo is the best teacher in the whole school," Lara confided proudly. "I wanted to be in her class, but the principal wouldn't let me 'cause we're family."

It wasn't polite to stare, Lara thought. Her mom said so. But Lara stared at the tall man anyway. She liked his face. It was strong but kind. He had great big hands, hands just right for holding.

"She's real pretty," Lara went on, toying with the end of her braid.

"Who is?" He looked confused.

"That girl you were with at school. She looks like the china doll my nana gave me last Christmas. It's not for playing with but just for looking at. Is she your kid?"

"Yes, she is. Her name's Tiffany." He smiled. Lara smiled back, liking the way he smiled with his dark blue eyes as well as his mouth.

"I'm eight."

"So is Tiffany."

"Does she have a best friend?"

Lara had lots of friends, but she didn't have a very best friend who liked her better than anybody else. It would be fun to have a very best friend with a pretty name like Tiffany.

He stopped smiling and his eyes looked kind of

sad. "No, she doesn't. If your mother is home, I'd like to talk to her."

"Okay. Come on."

Carter followed the little girl and the Saint Bernard up to the house. He offered to wait on the porch, but Lara invited him inside. She left him and the dog in the living room while she went out into the hall and yelled, "Hey, Mom! Moooom!"

The Saint Bernard sat on his haunches, lustfully eyeing Carter's shoelaces.

"Don't even think about it," he warned, moving away from the animal.

He didn't have anything against dogs per se. He just didn't care for the way they chewed up shoes, drooled, licked, scratched, shed hair, and generally destroyed one's house and nerves.

Glancing around the living room, he started, thinking the room had been ransacked by burglars. Then he realized it was simply in disarray and jam-packed with . . . stuff.

There were two sofas in shades of blue and sand, sand-colored chairs, teak bookcases, and an enormous old mahogany desk. Photographs littered tabletops. Mechanical toys, the collectors' kind that ought to be properly displayed, were scattered haphazardly. Trophies shared space with oriental vases and little boxes in silver and gold.

The ugliest artwork he'd ever seen hung on the walls, and there was an awful lot of it. He shuddered and deliberately focused on something else —an empty bird cage and a huge teddy bear that sat on a drop-leaf cherry table. The bear looked depressed in its ragged tutu and chewed-up ballet slippers.

The dog barked. Carter glanced over his shoulder and saw that Lara was standing behind him. She was studying him as thoroughly as he'd inspected the room. He wondered if he was making a better impression on her than the untidy room made on him.

He smiled. She smiled back, showing a slight gap in the center of her lower pearly whites. Grasping for a conversation starter, he gestured to the teddy bear and asked, "Does your bear have a name?"

"Her name is Sally. But she isn't mine. She's Happy's woman. Mom got her for him when he was a puppy so he wouldn't you-know-what on people's legs."

A dog's mistress, Carter thought. No wonder the bear looked depressed. He spared a pained glance at the Saint Bernard, who was happily chewing and drooling on one of Lara's shoelaces.

"I forgot to ask," she said. "What's your name?"

"Carter Dalton."

"I'm very pleased to meet you, Mr. Dalton." She said it so prim and proper, he had to smile.

"The pleasure is all mine, Miss Johnson."

She giggled, obviously delighted with the adult formality.

"Lara, have you seen the panties that go with this bra? Oh, my goodness!"

Carter looked up and over Lara's head. A woman stood in the doorway, a startled expression on her face, a black lace bra dangling from her fingertips.

She was small. He guessed she was barely a whisper of an inch over five feet tall and probably weighed in at one hundred pounds. Nothing about her looked a minute over eighteen, except for the maturity he saw in the brown eyes that dominated her plain face. No, "plain" wasn't quite right. She was pixie-cute, like Lara. Her hair was dark brown, baby-fine and shoulder-length.

She wore sweat-dampened athletic clothes— gray shorts, pink T-shirt, aerobic shoes, and socks. No jewelry except for an inexpensive wristwatch.

Shifting his perspective, he regarded the bra dangling from her hand. A skinny, sweaty woman holding a lacy bit of black fabric shouldn't have been sexy. But *she* was. He felt himself growing uncomfortably warm.

"Mrs. Johnson?" he said, schooling his expression into something more appropriate than sexual awareness.

"Oh, yes. That's me. My goodness," she repeated, laughing and shooting her daughter a quick glance. "I didn't realize we had company."

"Mom, remember the new girl I told you about?" Lara beamed a smile back at her mother. "The one in Aunt Mo's class at school? Her name is Tiffany. Isn't that a pretty name? He's Tiffany's daddy."

"I'm Carter Dalton." He stepped forward, his hand outstretched.

She raised her right hand. It happened to be the one holding the bra. She stared blankly at it. He inspected the feminine item, too, with more interest than was polite.

She choked out another laugh as she met his gaze. Carter found himself liking the infectious sound and the flush of pink staining her cheeks.

"Here, Lara." She handed her the garment. "Go put this in my room for me, sweetie."

"Okay." Lara fitted the bra over her eyes like goggles and peered up at her mother through the lace cups. "Want me to look for your panties too?"

The look on the woman's face was priceless. Carter pressed his lips together to hold back laughter.

"Uh, sure. Take Happy with you."

"Okay. Come on, Happy." Lara skipped off, twirling the sexy underwear by a strap. The dog romped beside her, snapping at the tail end of the bra.

Carter fought a grin—unsuccessfully. It was impossible not to feel good around that pixie of a little girl. She was so refreshingly open and natural.

Jenny gave him a chagrined look and shrugged. "Kids. Couldn't you just die sometimes?"

"Your daughter is adorable," he said sincerely.

"Shall we start over? Hi, I'm Jenny Johnson."

"Hello." As he shook her hand, his heart experienced a little jump start. She wasn't his type, he told himself. She was too small; the top of her head reached no higher than his chest. Too thin, although she did have great legs and a tiny waist a man could span with his hands. And too cute.

So why did he feel an instant, unnerving attraction to her? He gazed down at her and found a possible answer in her eyes. Fringed with thick dark lashes, her eyes had a life of their own. They sparkled as if she might burst out laughing at the least provocation. He found that quite appealing. There had been so little laughter in his life these past months.

"Well," she said, "what can I do for you, Mr. Dalton?"

He reluctantly released her hand, surprised at himself for feeling that reluctance. "Maureen Robbins suggested I contact you. I'd like to talk to you about—"

"Stop right there." She shook her head and held up her hand. "Look, Mr. Dalton, regardless of what Maureen may have told you, I'm not interested in going out with you. Nothing personal, you understand. I just don't date."

Piqued, he opened his mouth to speak and quickly closed it again. He'd almost blurted out, "Why not? What's wrong with me?" The emotional exhaustion of the last eight months must be taking a toll on his logic, he decided.

"I'm not here to ask you for a date."

She blinked at him. "You're not?"

"Uh, no."

Her hands flew up to cover her cheeks. "Boy, is my face red. Sorry about that. When you mentioned my sister, I assumed Mo was trying to set me up again. She's been trying to find me a husband ever since the ink dried on my divorce papers."

"No apology necessary. My mother used to do that to me all the time," he confided, doing his best to relieve her embarrassment.

"Used to? How did you convince her to stop?"

"I moved away."

"Oh?" She slanted a curious glance up at him. "Well, that's a bit too drastic for me. I was raised here, and I can't imagine living anywhere else now that I've settled here again. Maureen may be a pain in the neck sometimes, but she is my sister and my best friend. My parents retired and moved to Florida last year. I miss them like crazy."

Her wistful expression made him think of his own family, and he felt a twinge of wistfulness too. He quickly shook it off. As much as he loved and missed his parents, he'd done the right thing in putting some distance between them and their well-intentioned interference in his and Tiffany's lives.

"You really don't date?" he asked. Totally against his will, he could feel his interest in her growing stronger by the minute.

"Nope."

"Never?" His eyebrows inched upward.

"I gave it up for Lent, Mr. Dalton."

Cute and sassy. He smiled. "I've seen your underwear. That alone ought to put us on a first name basis."

"Fair enough." She smiled back, blushing prettily.

Breath caught in his throat. How could a smile be both guileless and sexy at the same time? And when that wide mouth of hers, with its soft and lush lips, shaped into a smile, her plain face was elevated to an appealing beauty.

"I really am sorry I jumped to the wrong conclusion, Carter. What can I do for you?"

He called upon his store of self-discipline to control his fascination with her eyes and her mouth. "Mrs. Robbins is my daughter's teacher. I had a conference with her today, and she recommended that I talk to you about the Sunshine Girls Club."

What a voice he had, Jenny thought, listening to the deep, rich baritone sound. He was certainly a tall one, so tall that she felt even shorter than she was standing next to him. He had a strong nose and mouth, a tiny cleft in his chin, and eyes so blue, they were almost the color of cobalt. Strands of silver threaded through his black hair, giving him a distinguished air of maturity. She placed his age in the upper thirty range. And he was dressed to polished perfection in a pin-striped suit, which made her feel a bit self-conscious about her grubby state.

"Oh, then you're a single parent," she said, darting a glance at his left hand. There was no ring on his finger, not even a faint white mark to show one had been there recently.

"Yes, I am. If you have time now, I'd like to know more about the club."

"Certainly. Please, sit down."

"Thank you."

As she walked over to one of the sofas, Jenny wondered why she suddenly felt so nervous around him. She busied herself for a moment, gathering up a blanket, pillow, and the morning newspaper, and dumping them into a nearby chair.

Still disturbed by the curious effect she had on him, Carter sat at the far end of the sofa, saying, "I hope I haven't caught you at a bad time. I tried all afternoon to call you, but whoever answered the phone kept hanging up on me. So I decided to drop by here on my way home from work."

"Lara and I were at the YMCA this afternoon," she said. "I teach step aerobics there three days a week while Lara takes gymnastic lessons. So you must have talked to T-Beau."

"Is T-Beau a child?"

Jenny laughed. "No. He's older than I am, I think. T-Beau is a parrot."

Carter gave her a strange look. "I talked to a *parrot*?"

"He's learned how to use the speaker phone in

the kitchen," she explained. "African gray parrots are the best talkers in the parrot world."

He regarded her with a dubious expression. She didn't blame him.

"One has to experience T-Beau before believing he is intelligent enough to answer a telephone."

"I see." Carter's voice was very polite.

"How long have you been a single parent?" she asked, steering the conversation back on course.

"Tiffany's mother died eight months ago. Carol and I had been divorced for two years before—" He stopped speaking abruptly as though he hadn't meant to tell her that.

"Ah, then you're fairly new at this single-parent business. Overwhelming at times, isn't it?"

"You can say that again." He broke into an open, friendly smile. "Tiffany is my only child. I didn't grow up with sisters, so I'm operating on pure instinct."

"Believe me, that's all any of us can do." She swallowed a bubble of nervous laughter. "What did Maureen tell you about the club?"

"Only that it was a club for girls being raised by single parents." His gaze traveled over her from head to toe. "I wouldn't have guessed you and Mrs. Robbins were sisters."

Jenny sighed inwardly, knowing he was thinking how different she was from her sister. A man like him probably had tall, beautiful blondes like Mo falling all over him.

She felt certain his only motive in seeking her out was to inquire about the Sunshine Girls Club. Unfortunately for him, she suspected her sister's motive for sending him to her weren't as pure.

Carter Dalton was the perfect example of the type of man Maureen loved to throw in her path: handsome, mature, and upwardly mobile. No, she suspected her sister had a hidden agenda that the poor man wasn't aware of.

She also knew that divorced or widowed men with children were often more quick to remarry than women in the same circumstances. Had Maureen sensed he was on the prowl for a wife?

"About the club." Her voice had a husky sound to it. She cleared her throat and started over. "It's an informal support group, more or less."

God, she was little, Carter thought. He felt big and clumsy next to her. It was craziness, but he wanted to get lost in her sparkling eyes and find out if her mouth was as soft and sweet as it looked.

Forget it, he commanded himself. Thinking about kissing Jenny Johnson was way out of bounds. His only reason for being there was to get his daughter involved with the Sunshine Girls. He forced himself to concentrate on what she was saying.

"The club is relatively new. Emily, my coleader, and I just started it in January. There are seven members, ages eight to ten, including my daughter. We meet every Saturday morning at the Battleground Recreation Center."

He made an effort to keep his gaze fixed on her eyes and not her mouth. "Are you a psychologist or a trained counselor?"

She smiled. "No. I'm a church secretary, and I teach step aerobics at the YMCA."

He wondered if she had any idea how sensual her voice sounded to him.

"I don't have any qualifications for leading a support group," she continued. "I'm just a concerned parent who saw a need in my daughter and some of her friends that wasn't being met. There are plenty of support groups to help divorced and widowed adults over the rough times, but very few, if any, for children. I decided to do something about it."

He wasn't personally interested in her, Carter reminded himself when she stopped speaking and stared curiously at him. Then he realized she was waiting for him to say something.

"That's very commendable," he said. "Support groups have never interested me one way or the other. But I suppose—"

"Braaak! Off with your head!"

The sweet childlike voice seemed to come out of nowhere. Startled, Carter looked around. He saw a parrot swoop into the room, aiming straight for his head.

TWO

Carter ducked as the parrot circled over his head, ruffling his hair. "What is that? An attack bird?"

Jenny grinned. "Don't be frightened. That's T-Beau. He's just playing."

Oh sure, Carter thought, that's what Lara had said about the hundred-and-fifty-pound Saint Bernard. Playful old Happy had rushed at him as though the word "dinner" had been stamped across his forehead. Carter automatically flinched and drew back as the parrot swooped past him once more.

Jenny laughed and said indulgently, "Behave yourself, you vampire bat. Our guest doesn't appreciate your birdy games."

"Braaak!" The parrot perched on the sofa arm beside her. "Now tell the truth. Did you ever eat a bat?"

"Silly bird." She laughed again and stroked his head with her fingertips.

"Awwwk. Pretty bird."

Pretty it was not, Carter thought. Its body was gunmetal gray with random splotches the color of dried blood, which was also the color of its stubby tail.

"Amazing," he said. "That's the voice I heard on the phone." His initial shock was wearing off. "That bird actually talks. It really answers the telephone."

"*He,*" she corrected. "African grays aren't the most beautiful of parrots, but they are very intelligent." She smiled apologetically. "I've been meaning to get rid of the speaker phone in the kitchen ever since T-Beau learned how to use it."

Carter frowned. "How smart is he? Does he really know what he's saying?"

"I've read that the gray parrot can reason symbolically like a chimpanzee," she answered, still stroking T-Beau's feathers. "He can pick out shapes, colors, and can tell you the names of his toys. However, I doubt that he really understands the concept of everything he says."

The parrot flexed its wings and took to the air. It landed on the coffee table.

Jenny smiled fondly at her pet, even though the creature was pushing magazines off the table. "Studies have shown that parrots have the emotional development of a three-year-old child. That's what T-Beau acts like most of the time, a naughty toddler."

Carter nodded, and wondered how one disciplined a naughty bird. He bent down and began picking up the magazines nearest his feet on the floor. When he straightened, he found himself the object of an intense parrot scrutiny.

"Braaak! Bugger off, sissy boy." T-Beau cocked his head this way and that, evidently quite pleased with himself.

"Same to you, fella." Carter squelched the urge to smack the insulting bird with the magazines.

"T-Beau, go to your cage," Jenny said firmly.

"No." The parrot turned its back on her. Just like a sulky toddler, Carter thought wryly.

"Go!" Jenny ordered, clapping her hands together.

"Awwwk! Don't bother me."

"That's what he said to me every time I called," Carter said.

"Sorry about that. T-Beau has warped ideas about what constitutes acceptable conversation."

"Are there any other exotic pets lurking about?" he asked as he absently sorted the magazines he held. *House Beautiful* went on top of *Parents*. "I'm beginning to feel like I'm in a carnival fun house, waiting for something else unexpected to pop out at me."

"No. You're safe. The rest are quite ordinary."

"The rest?" He glanced up to see laughter sparkling in her brown eyes. He found himself automatically smiling in response.

"Three cats, two gerbils, some tropical fish. Don't worry. The cats are outside. The gerbils are in their cage—I hope—up in Lara's room. And to my knowledge the fish have never escaped from the aquarium."

In Carter's opinion, Jenny was a tad on the messy, pack-rat side and she had far too many animals. But on the positive side, she had a "feel good" voice and a spontaneous sense of humor. She was definitely worth getting to know.

The parrot said something, then flew over to its cage, grumbling to itself in a language Carter didn't recognize.

"What did he say?" Carter eyed the bird suspiciously.

She shrugged. "Beats me. I don't understand Cajun French. T-Beau knows quite a few words and phrases in that language. All of them rude and colorful, or so Aunt Charlotte claimed."

"Cajun French?" He stared at her. Surely she was putting him on.

She nodded. "My aunt won T-Beau in a poker game off a transvestite Creole cook. The cook had owned him for many years, and according to Charlotte, he was a bad influence on T-Beau. She attempted to give T-Beau a little class by teaching him to recite lines from her favorite book, *Alice's Adventures in Wonderland.*"

Carter shook his head slightly as he leaned down to pick up a copy of *Cricket* magazine off the table. He wasn't going to ask. He didn't want to know. But curiosity was killing him.

"I hate to be nosy," he finally said. "But how

did your aunt come to know a transvestite Creole cook?"

Jenny laughed. "He was a neighbor of hers in the French Quarter in New Orleans. Charlotte was an eccentric free spirit and an artist. When she died a few years ago, I inherited T-Beau and many of her paintings. That's her work on the wall behind you, and over there, and there."

He scanned the badly executed paintings of French Quarter scenes and heads of famous people: a sequined Elvis in his hefty stage and Marilyn Monroe in her famous stance over an air vent, to name a few.

He dropped his gaze. "They're, uh . . ." He plucked *Time* magazine off the table and filed it into place with the others in his lap. "Your aunt's work is . . . I've never seen such . . ." He gave her a helpless smile.

She folded her arms. He knew she was trying not to smile. She didn't succeed. "You don't have to be nice. I know they're awful paintings. Charlotte lacked taste and talent in her chosen profession, but she pursued it with joy and energy anyway."

"If you know her work is . . . awful, why do you display it?"

"Because I loved her dearly," she answered in a matter-of-fact tone.

Carter stared at her for a long moment. She returned his stare openly, and he wondered if she found him as interesting—and as puzzling—as he found her. For the first time he noticed the sprinkling of freckles across the bridge of her nose. Once again, he revised his opinion. The more he looked at her face, the more attractive she became.

Jenny caught her breath at the sudden flare of sexual interest in those cobalt eyes of his. To her dismay, she felt an unnerving response deep within her feminine core. She had never experienced such a startling rush of sensuality from simply gazing into a man's eyes.

Acutely aware of how absurd it was to desire the kiss of a stranger, she forced herself back to reality, lowering her gaze to his hands. "Do you realize that you've alphabetized my magazines?" she asked distractedly.

"Yes. It's a habit. I'm an organizational development consultant."

She gave him a blank look.

"I specialize in motion and time studies," he explained. "Companies hire me to improve human effectiveness, to improve productivity and efficiency."

"How, uh, nice."

Jenny equated efficiency experts with perfectionists. Both gave her a pain. Her ex-husband had been an impossible perfectionist. She'd never been able to please him, and after a while, she'd just stopped trying.

Carter neatly placed the alphabetized magazines on the coffee table. "What do the Sunshine Girls do at their meetings?"

She blinked twice at the rapid conversational switch. How strange, she mused. For a while she'd forgotten his purpose in being there.

"We do something different at every meeting," she said. "Crafts, learn new skills, play games, take field trips. We've had guests come talk to the girls on various subjects such as bicycle safety. And at every meeting we have a friendship circle where the girls can talk about anything they want."

His mouth turned down in a slight grimace. "You mean, they talk about their feelings?"

A shadow darkened his eyes. She wondered if he was uncomfortable with the oral expression of emotions, his own or his daughter's.

"If they want to," she said.

His brows drew together in a frown.

She hastened to add, "Sharing with others going through a similar crisis is extremely helpful. It doesn't necessarily solve your problems, but it drastically cuts down on loneliness and the feeling that you're the only one who has ever experienced what you're going through."

He studied her face for a long moment. Jenny wasn't surprised to catch a shrewd, measuring look in his serious eyes. She had a feeling it was his nature to weigh, measure, and categorize everything. Since she was the extreme opposite, she decided it was a very good thing that she didn't have a personal interest in him.

"What are your objectives?" he asked.

"Club objectives?" She nibbled on her lower

lip. That was a tricky question to answer. "Most of the time I operate on pure instinct. I guess you could say I fly by the seat of my pants from one meeting to the next."

"I see."

His obvious disapproval, or perhaps it was disappointment, made her feel defensive. It had been a long time since she had allowed a man to make her feel that way, and she resented it.

"Let me explain something here." She folded her arms and met his gaze straight on. "All of my girls have experienced either the death of a parent or a parent's divorce, which has punched holes in their adult support system and in their self-esteem. Children, like adults, need a support system, a network of caring individuals with whom they can experience acceptance of thoughts, feelings, and the value of his or her being. That's what I hope the club can be for my girls: a nurturing support system."

Carter didn't fail to notice the warm glow that lit up her eyes or the caring attitude she conveyed in those two little words: *my girls*. Nor did he miss the take-it-or-leave-it way she was now looking at him.

Behind her pixie exterior was a capable mind, a heart full of benevolence, and a measure of stubborn pride. She intrigued him in more ways than he cared to examine. That was something he had not expected at the outset of his inquiry.

"I don't believe," she added, "that rigid structure and set objectives are necessary. As I said, we're a support group."

"I disagree."

Amazing, he thought, how pretty she became with a little fire in her eyes. He decided to make a deliberate push to see if he could turn up the heat. "Structure and objectives are important in any group."

It worked, but only briefly. She doused the flames and her expression smoothed out as she said calmly, "If that's what you think your daughter needs, maybe you should try another organization. The Girl Scouts have plenty of objectives. Your daughter could earn badges for everything from cooking to wilderness backpacking."

Carter watched her carefully for a moment. "Why do I get the impression you're trying to discourage me?"

"Your intuition is missing the mark." She seemed to be looking through his eyes and into his head, gauging what made him tick. "I just thought you might be happier enrolling your daughter in a more structured organization."

Carter lapsed into his own private thoughts. Worried thoughts as he considered what Jenny had said about the importance of a child's personal support network. His daughter's personal support network had been torn apart. First by the divorce of her parents, second by her mother's sudden death. Guilt settled uneasily on him as he now considered the move away from family and friends in

Georgia as further destruction of Tiffany's support system.

He quickly made up his mind. "I believe the concept of the Sunshine Girls Club is more suitable for my daughter at this time." Hearing the strain in his voice, he modified his tone. "With your permission, I'd like to bring my daughter to one of your meetings. Of course, I'd want to observe the group before making a final decision to enroll her in the club."

"Mr. Dalton," she said hesitantly.

"Carter."

She smiled faintly at the reminder. "I've kind of promised my coleader I wouldn't take on any new club members at this time. Our regular meetings end with the school year. That's only six weeks away. We'd be delighted to have Tiffany join us when school starts up in the fall."

That wasn't what Carter wanted to hear. "But that's almost six months from now."

She lifted her hand in an apologetic gesture. "I'm sorry. Emily thinks we already have our hands full with the girls we have. The group is relatively new, and we're still in the process of getting comfortable with one another."

Carter felt his chest constrict. He reached out and took one of her hands in his. His action startled her, he saw that, but no more than it did him. He wasn't one to touch women in so casual a manner, especially one he'd just met.

She laughed. "Mr. Dalton."

"Carter," he reminded her again. "Did anyone ever tell you that you have a nice laugh, Jenny? I find myself smiling every time I hear it."

The non sequitur threw Jenny off balance. The static electricity that seemed to flow from his hand to hers made her stare warily at him. She wiggled her fingers as a hint for him to let go. He didn't take the hint.

"Are you uncomfortable with compliments?" he asked. "Or is it that you're uncomfortable with me?" He ran his fingers over her wrist. "Your palm is damp. Your pulse is fast."

She met his gaze levelly and hoped she managed to look amused rather than shaken. "Are you perchance sucking up to me?"

"No." He smiled and released her hand. "But I'm not proud. I will, if that's what it takes."

She couldn't resist his smile. "Then you'd better do some major sucking up to Emily. Want her phone number?"

There was a light in his eyes she hadn't noticed before. It was a tease, a laugh, and very appealing. "I'd rather suck up to you."

"You don't look like that kind of man."

"I'm not usually. But you're talking to a desperate father. My daughter needs the Sunshine Girls now. Tiffany needs someone like you to teach her how to laugh again."

That last statement got to Jenny in a way no flattery ever would. Emily would kill her, but she knew she was going to cave in. There was a soft spot in her heart for concerned daddies, especially since Lara's father was too busy indulging in his second youth to be bothered with his own child.

Apparently taking her silence for continued hesitation, he said, "May I be candid with you, Jenny?"

"Certainly."

"Tiffany and I just moved here in February. She's having trouble adjusting to the move and she still hasn't recovered from the shock of her mother's death."

"I'm sorry," she said. She would have liked to offer something more supportive, but she couldn't tell by looking at him if it would be welcome. If eyes were the windows to the soul, his were shuttered and locked.

He just nodded and continued in a voice that gave none of his feelings away. "Tiffy has always been a quiet and shy child. She's only eight, like your daughter. Now she's . . . withdrawn and silent. She isn't making friends at school or in the neighborhood." He avoided Jenny's eyes. "I'm worried about her."

"It's normal for a child to feel abandoned when a parent dies," she said gently. "Sometimes they withdraw from the people around them as a means of protecting themselves from being hurt again."

"Your sister said that too. That's why she thinks the Sunshine Girls would help Tiffany."

He looked at her. This time the shutters were open slightly, and she saw a hint of genuine emotion in his eyes. "I know it's important to keep promises, Jenny. I wouldn't ask you to break one under ordinary circumstances. But please, couldn't you make an exception for my little girl?"

He reached for her hand again. She swallowed hard, dangerously aware of the warmth of his big hands, their gentle strength. "Would you really turn away a lonely, friendless child who needs you and your support group?"

Jenny knew perfectly well that he was deliberately playing on her emotions. "I—" She laughed and shook her head. "Carter, has anyone ever told *you* that you're a shameless manipulator?"

His eyebrows crept upward. "Is it working?"

"Of course. I'm not heartless."

He smiled. "According to Mrs. Robbins, you're the most compassionate person she knows."

"What she meant is that I'm a soft touch," she responded with asperity. All too conscious of the way her hand fit so well in his, she eased away and locked her hands together in her lap.

"Soft touch. Soft voice. Soft heart. A wonderful laugh. You're just what my daughter needs." His words and the warm expression in his eyes weakened her knees and totally melted her resolve.

Jenny sighed. In spite of his manipulativeness, she was certain he'd been honest about his situation. If they were going to deal with each other, she'd best be honest with him in return.

"Carter, I'm going to level with you. The Sunshine Girls aren't the Girl Scouts. In fact, all but a couple of my girls are Girl Scout rejects. Don't laugh, I'm serious. I was the assistant leader of the troop that JoJo, Margaret, and Kamika were kicked out of in November."

"What did they do?"

"Nothing terrible, really. They're good kids. They just have problems and they tend to act up."

"My daughter has a problem. But if you refuse to help her . . ." A martyred look of resignation entered his expression as he stood up and looked down at her. "I'm sorry to have bothered you. Thank you for listening to a distraught father."

Jenny made a face as she rose to her feet. "Cut it out, Carter. I didn't say Tiffany couldn't join the club. I'm only trying to tell you that my girls can be a bit rowdy."

His smile was condescending. She resisted the temptation to sock him.

"I'm sure they're all wonderful children like your Lara," he said.

Never turn away from the truth, she thought, even if it embarrassed you. "Wonderful, yes. But some of them are, uh, wild. Emily raised two children of her own, and she swears nothing less than frontline combat could have prepared her for JoJo, Kamika, and Margaret."

He laughed as though she'd just told an exceptionally funny joke. His expression said, "They're little girls. How wild and rowdy could they be?"

Jenny shook her head in resignation. "Bring

Tiffany to our meeting tomorrow morning at the Battleground Recreation Center."

"Great. What time?" His smile warmed. It caused uncomfortably exciting things to her pulse rate.

"Nine-fifteen." The meeting actually began at nine. Jenny hoped fifteen minutes would be enough time for the girls to blow off steam before the Daltons arrived.

"Should she bring anything special?"

"No. Have her wear play clothes, ones that won't matter if she gets them dirty."

"Okay. Thank you, Jenny. You'll never know how much this means to Tiffany and me."

As she walked with him out to the foyer, she wondered if he would still be so thankful after he met her girls.

At the front door, he stood looking down at her for a moment. Then he said softly, "I really meant it, you know."

"Meant what?"

"Your laughter makes me smile."

Jenny refused to take him seriously in spite of the serious intensity in his expression. "Well, you know what they say about smiling. It increases your face value."

"Then I believe my face value has skyrocketed," he said, smiling down at her.

Butterflies danced in her stomach. "Well, I . . . It was nice meeting you."

"I look forward to seeing you tomorrow, Jenny." He lifted one hand to her cheek. It rested lightly there, then his fingers inched upward to tuck her hair behind her ear. The lingering caress created confusion and an unsettling sensation in her.

She willed her weakened knees to hold her upright. "See you tomorrow."

Minutes later, Jenny sat alone on the stairs. She thought about the feel of his fingers on her face and the faint smell of his spicy, masculine cologne. It confused her.

I am not attracted to that man. I imagined it.

Half-dazed, she realized she would have to see him every time he brought his daughter to a Sunshine Girls meeting. Nerves fluttered in her throat at the thought. Her mind raced on with her heartbeat as she finally conceded that she hadn't imagined the stirring of attraction. She sighed and rubbed her clammy hands on the hips of her shorts.

"It's nothing to get excited about," she whispered, then bit her lip. In all probability, the feeling would pass through her system quicker than an annoying head cold. Until it did pass, she vowed to maintain only a friendly attitude toward Carter Dalton.

But before she had to face him again tomorrow morning, she was going to call Maureen and find out exactly what she was up to.

Saturday morning the Sunshine Girls were in rare form. Jenny sat on the floor, watching them buzz around the activity room as though they'd ingested a truckload of sugar. When the kids were wound up this tight, she reasoned that the only sane thing to do was to let them wear themselves out.

JoJo, the club's leading instigator of mischief, was racing around, making like an airplane with her arms thrown out to the sides. "I don't know but I've been told, air force wings are made of gold," she sang over and over. She was thin and wiry, tall for her age, and she had grayish-green eyes set in an intense face. Her spiky blond hair was hidden beneath an old baseball cap, and she wore her father's Desert Storm camouflage shirt over her jeans, which were torn at the knees.

JoJo was rough around the edges, and her mouth constantly got her into trouble at home and at school. Jenny had a soft spot for the girl nonetheless. She often thought that if JoJo had been a boy and lived a few centuries ago, she would have gone about with her sword drawn, looking for dragons to slay and battles to win.

Across the room, Kamika pounded on the keyboard of an old upright piano. A slim, supple creature with copper skin, she always wore designer kids' clothes and gold beads braided into her black hair. Jenny knew that her mother had just gone through a tough divorce and was so caught up in finding a job and straightening out her own life, she didn't have much time or energy for Kamika. Unfortunately, that seemed to reinforce the child's negative attitude and tendency to complain about everything.

"Let's make a ballet!" Sarah cried, dancing over to Kamika. She spun around, performing an arabesque, her leg suspended in the air behind her. Sarah wasn't a pretty child, but something about her commanded a second look. Her naturally curly red hair hung like a mantle around her face, and her eyes were a deep, clear blue. She was a whirl-wind, rarely still for long.

JoJo rushed over to join them. "Yeah, a ballet. We can call it 'The Waltz of the Morons.' " She and Sarah did three rapid spins, which made them so dizzy, they fell on the floor, giggling.

Jenny's gaze drifted over to Lara and Cheryl. Lara was trying to teach Cheryl how to do a cart-wheel, but the pudgy child kept falling on her fanny. Jenny swallowed a sigh. She worried about all the girls, but she worried about Cheryl the most. She was an odd child with brown eyes that reflected a depth of anxiety that no eight-year-old should know. Overweight. Oversensitive. She clung to any adult who showed her the least bit of attention.

The frenetic activity, the constantly rising noise level, didn't concern Jenny. At the moment she was more concerned about her coleader.

She glanced at the woman sitting beside her. A lovely lady in her early sixties, Emily bore a close resemblance to the actress Helen Hayes. She was kind and soft-spoken, but a mite on the nervous side. When their young charges acted up, she didn't cope well, and today she appeared more shell-shocked than usual. Her left eye was twitching rapidly, making her look like a rather demented Helen Hayes.

Not a good sign, Jenny thought. As she returned her attention to the activity going on around them, she saw an airborne purple tennis shoe heading straight for her and Emily.

"Duck!" she yelped as she leaned back. The canvas missile whizzed by her nose. It sailed over Emily's head, missing her by a mere inch, and hit the floor a few feet away.

"That does it!" Emily uncurled and raised up on her knees.

"Sorry," Bunny giggled, rushing over to grab the shoe.

"Sorry," Margaret echoed, attempting to take the purple tennis shoe away from her friend.

The Impossible Twins was what Jenny had dubbed those two. They looked a little alike. Both were short, with light brown hair and brown eyes. They were both aggressive and always ready to brawl.

The two girls squealed and giggled as they fought over the tennis shoe. Margaret won possession and took off running. Bunny was right behind her.

"I can't take it anymore," Emily wailed. "They're out to get us."

Jenny patted her shoulder. "No, they're not. They're just blowing off a little steam."

"They *are* out to get us. I've had gum spat in my hair, and—"

"That was an accident," Jenny quickly interjected. "It isn't at all noticeable where we had to cut the gum out."

"I've been wrapped up like a mummy."

"You volunteered to let them practice first aid on you. The girls just got a little overenthusiastic, that's all."

"Did I volunteer to be locked in the supply closet?"

Jenny averted her gaze from Emily's stern glare. "It really wasn't their fault that the key broke off in the lock and we had to get a locksmith to get you out."

"No matter what they do, you always defend them. I tell you, they're out of control little monsters. Now, you want to add another one to this motley crew." Emily sliced one hand across her throat. "I've had it up to here. I'm sorry, but I quit."

Alarmed, Jenny got to her knees. "You don't mean that, Em. Please, you can't quit."

Emily slowly stood up. "Oh, yes I can. I don't have a daughter in this club. My children are grown. With any luck, they'll remain single and childless."

"Please, the girls need you. *I* need you. Give them another chance to—"

A hundred pounds of baby fat tackled Jenny. The rest of her plea was knocked out of her along with her breath as she was plopped back on her fanny. Emily made good her escape as Jenny gasped for air and tried to free herself from Cheryl's loving stranglehold.

"Where's Miz Smith going?" Cheryl yelled in her ear.

"Home. You're choking me, sweetie."

The child loosened her grip a little and drew back to peer anxiously at Jenny. "Ain't she coming back?"

"I don't think so."

"*Food fight!*" The voice that rose above the noise belonged to JoJo.

Eyes popping open, Jenny saw a shower of raisins coming her way.

THREE

Carter was having second thoughts as he escorted his daughter to her first Sunshine Girl meeting. It would be so easy to get back in the car and go home. Then no one would ever know that his stomach was tied in knots or that a cold sweat threatened to break out across his forehead.

If anyone had bothered to notice, they would have seen a composed, though slightly preoccupied man, wearing a teal-blue shirt and jeans so crisp, one would suspect he'd just walked out of the store with them. They would have seen a petite girl in a pretty pink sundress tightly clutching his hand.

All through breakfast Carter had spouted jovial nonsense about the joys of being a Sunshine Girl, about how exciting it was to start something new, about how much fun she was going to have making new friends. Big talk, hotshot, he berated himself. Tiffany was giving the silent, suffering impression she was on her way to being shot without benefit of a last McDonald's Happy Meal.

"Daddy?"

He looked down at her. She was white as a sheet. "You okay, Tiffy?"

"I'm scared."

He swore silently, then put on a smile. "There's nothing to be scared about." He gave her tiny fingers a reassuring squeeze.

"But what if they don't like me?"

"They'll like you. You're the greatest kid in the whole wide world."

Her lips curved a bit, but her eyes remained doubtful.

They walked on to the front entrance of the building. As they neared the door, it flew open and a silvery-haired woman shot out. She looked as though a Doberman pinscher was snapping at her heels.

"Don't go in there!" the lady warned breathlessly.

Carter stared at her. "I beg your pardon?"

She just shook her head and hurried away.

He stood for a second and wondered what that was all about. Feeling perplexed and more wary than ever, he ushered his daughter into the building.

The piercing sounds of shouts, screams, and laughter echoed in the corridor. Carter winced. The noise seemed to be coming from a room at the far end of the long hallway.

Surely, he thought, that couldn't be the Sunshine Girls. Little girls couldn't generate that much noise. Could they?

He felt Tiffany's grip on his hand tighten. Was it because of his hesitation or because of the noise? He glanced at her and smiled again, with more encouragement than he felt. "Sounds like somebody's having fun, huh?"

A sense of dread prickled at the back of his neck as they walked toward the calliope of children's voices. Jenny had warned him that the girls were a bit rowdy. He'd dismissed that, choosing to believe she simply exaggerated the facts. Now he was wondering if there was some truth in her claim that his shy little girl might find the other kids overwhelming.

One glance inside the room at the end of the hall and Carter's mouth dropped open. It seemed everywhere he looked were girls of every shape and size imaginable. Everywhere he looked, he saw arms, legs, mouths, and . . . *food* in motion.

Good God, he thought. The little demons were pelting one another with cookies and raisins.

Shifting his gaze, he saw a red-haired moppet dancing on a piano bench, while another kid pounded the keyboard of the old upright piano. In voices shrill enough to wake the dead, they belted out a verse of "Ninety-nine Bottles of Beer on the Wall."

Carter's preconceived notions about the club and its members crumbled faster than the cookies hitting the floor. His vision of sweet angels playing with dolls, sewing samplers, quietly discussing "girl" things, visiting elderly shut-ins, et cetera went south in a hurry.

He shuddered and drew Tiffany closer to his side. Whipping a glance about, he finally located Jenny. A hefty kid had her down on the floor in a headlock. An expression of helpless amusement was on Jenny's cute face as she watched the chaos going on around her.

Just when he thought he'd seen it all, the chubby girl picked something out of Jenny's hair and *ate* it!

Carter's stomach churned. His breakfast threatened to come back to haunt him.

He slipped a protective arm around his daughter's shoulders and glanced down at her. Tiffany looked so small, fragile, and innocent in her neat pink-and-white sundress and matching sweater. Her blue eyes were huge as she stared at the children. There was no doubt in his mind that his poor little darling was terrified right out of her lace anklets and snow-white Keds.

How could Jenny let those hellions get away with this kind of behavior? he wondered, appalled. His gaze sought her out again. Obviously, she was too softhearted, too good-natured to control them properly.

He really liked Jenny. Like? Hell, last night in bed, he'd had some wicked thoughts about her. He'd imagined what she would look like wearing that black lace bra and the missing panties. Even better, he'd imagined her wearing nothing but a smile.

Regret flowed through him. He just couldn't bring himself to leave Tiffany here with these out-of-control kids. Which meant he wouldn't be seeing Jenny every Saturday morning.

Carter considered gathering his daughter up and quietly backing out of the room. Before he could talk himself into that, his natural aversion to disorder overrode his inclination to run.

"Stay here, baby face," he ordered softly, and moved a few steps farther into the room.

"*Quiet!*" His shout was loud enough to be heard by every little ear in the place.

One by one, the girls froze. All eyes were suddenly focused on him.

He pointed to the child standing on the piano bench. "Get down."

He gestured to another kid. "And you, drop those cookies."

That wasn't quite the right thing to say, he realized belatedly as a handful of Oreos hit the floor.

He sternly eyed the children one by one until his gaze rested upon Jenny. "Now, would somebody please tell me what is going on here?"

No one moved. No one spoke.

Talk about bad timing, Jenny thought, staring up at Carter. *Perturbed* was too mild a word for the expression on his handsome face. Mr. Structure and Objectives stood there looking like a thundercloud waiting to shoot jagged bolts of lightning down on a parade.

Her heart sank to her toes. Any hope of her girls making a favorable impression upon him crashed and burned.

Then she became vividly aware of the silence. For once the Sunshine Girls were blissfully quiet. The only noise she heard was the collective sound of hers and Cheryl's breathing.

She looked around at the children. Carter might not be impressed by the girls, but they were certainly impressed by the authority in his voice and his commanding presence. She'd never seen them react so instantly to anyone, or be so quiet and still.

Amazing. Simply amazing.

A brilliant idea restored her heart to its rightful place. Carter would make an excellent coleader. She was admittedly disorganized, and she tended not to get too hung up on planning and order. As an efficiency expert, Carter possessed those qualities she lacked. Together, she decided, they just might strike a terrific balance between flexibility and structure.

That is, if she could talk him into it.

She pried Cheryl's fingers loose from her neck and nudged the child off her right leg. As she got to her feet, she discovered her leg was numb. Fixing a smile on her face, she limped over to greet the Daltons.

"Hi, Carter. You're right on time."

"Hello, Jenny." There was a slight edge in his voice. "Would you mind telling me what is going on here?"

She splayed her hands. "Oh, we're just blowing off a little steam."

His mouth turned down in disapproval. "With a food fight?"

She smiled brightly, determined not to let his disapproval put her on the defensive. "Sure. Haven't you ever had a food fight?"

"No."

"Too bad. It's lots of fun."

He didn't look convinced. In fact, he looked appalled that anyone over the age of three would think that.

Jenny shifted her perspective to regard the dark-haired princess of a little girl hugging the doorjamb behind her father. She skirted around Carter to take the child's hand in hers. "Hi, Tiffany. I'm Jenny Johnson. Welcome to the Sunshine Girls Club."

"Hello." Big eyes, eyes as blue as her father's, stared at Jenny for a second, then shied away.

"Would you like to go play with the other girls, while I talk to your father for a minute?" she said softly.

Tiffany's gaze darted to the children scattered about the room. A sad shadow of wistfulness crossed her sweet face. For a second, she looked like a hungry kid with her nose pressed against the window of a candy store: longing to go in but denied entrance by virtue of her empty pockets.

Jenny's heart went out to her. She wanted to pick her up and hug her until that shadowed expression faded.

"Jenny."

She felt Carter's brief touch upon her arm.

"I think we need to talk," he said.

"Of course," she answered, glancing at him. "But first, let me introduce you."

Not giving him a chance to protest, she quickly turned to face the curious girls watching them. "Girls, this is Mr. Dalton and his daughter, Tiffany. Say hello and make them feel welcome."

A few weak voices responded. A few raised hands waved limply.

Jenny swallowed a sigh. "Now that we've had our fun, it's time to clean up."

That announcement was met with groans and grimaces.

She put JoJo in charge of the cleanup detail, knowing that where JoJo led, the others would follow.

Delighted with the task, JoJo puffed up with importance. "All right, you morons," she said, hands on her hips. "Jenny says we gotta clean up this mess." She started issuing instructions in a manner that would have made her drill sergeant father proud.

Jenny called to Lara.

Clutching the purple tennis shoe that Margaret

thrust at her, Lara detached herself from the group and came running. She skidded to a halt with a breathless, "Hi-hi, Mr. Dalton."

"Hello." Carter's lips automatically curved in response to the charming imp smiling up at him.

He kept silent as Jenny introduced Lara to Tiffany. But when she told her daughter to introduce Tiffany to the rest of the group, he protested. "Wait a minute. I don't think—"

That was all he got out before his baby was taken by the hand and led away. He experienced a brief moment of panic.

"Come on, Carter, let's talk out in the hall."

He dragged his gaze away from his daughter and looked at Jenny. "Maybe we should talk right here."

"Don't worry. She'll be fine." Her sparkling brown eyes laughed up at him.

"But—"

"Lara will take care of her."

He wasn't so certain about that, but he reluctantly allowed Jenny to take his arm. He shot several glances over his shoulder at his daughter as he went through the doorway.

Just outside the door, he dug his heels in and stopped. Jenny gave him a questioning look. "I want to keep an eye on what's going on in there," he said firmly.

"All right." She released his arm and leaned back against the wall, studying him with apparent curiosity. "I guess the club isn't what you expected, huh?"

"No, it certainly isn't. Do these children always behave like that?"

"No. Sometimes they're much worse."

"Is that supposed to make me feel better?"

"No," she responded cheerfully. "Of course, sometimes they're much better than you've seen so far. Sometimes they're so sweet and adorable that I want to take them all home and keep them forever."

"Sweet and adorable?" He stared at her incredulously. "I like Lara, and I'm willing to believe that of her. But the rest of those hellions? No way."

"How do you do that?"

"Do what?"

"Arch one brow. I'm impressed." She tried it. "See, I can't do it without squinting one eye and looking ridiculous."

Carter caught himself starting to smile and quickly squelched it. "I won't be distracted from the subject."

Her own lips softened and curved. He was ridiculously tempted to move close, to touch her lips with a fingertip.

Damn. She could distract him without speaking a word.

He tore his gaze from her. Glancing over his shoulder into the room, he sought out his daughter. She seemed okay. No one was tripping her with a broom or throwing food at her. Lara was chatting away at her as she picked up broken cookies and tossed them into the trash can held by the chubby girl.

"Carter, stop looking over your shoulder. No one's going to intentionally hurt Tiffany."

"How about unintentionally?" he asked stiffly as he met her gaze again.

She sighed and shook her head. "You're going to have to get over being such a worrywart, if Tiffany is going to be a member of this group."

There was no *if* about it in his mind.

"By the way," she added, "you forgot to have Tiffany dress in play clothes."

He gave her a puzzled look and started to ask what was wrong with Tiffany's clothes, but thought better of it. The way his daughter was dressed was a moot point.

She wouldn't be joining the club.

As he decided how to tell Jenny he'd changed his mind about the club, his gaze traveled over her from scuffed sneakers to the jungle-print shirt half tucked into khaki shorts to the silky brunette hair framing her face. She was so darn cute, and so little. He didn't want to hurt her feelings. He wanted to . . .

Uncomfortable emotions rose to the surface as he acknowledged his powerful sexual awareness of her. Talk about bad timing. He didn't need that kind of thing in his life right now.

"I've changed my mind," he said tersely, taking refuge in anger. "I can't allow Tiffany to join the

Sunshine Girls. They're too wild. And you obviously can't control them."

That last statement came out more blatantly rude than he'd intended. He wasn't going to retract it, though. It was simply the truth as he saw it.

She smiled, seeming not the least bit offended. "You're right."

"I beg your pardon?" He hadn't expected her to agree with him, and it threw him off balance.

Her expression remained placid. "I'm too softhearted, too easygoing, and the girls know it. They need a leader whose authority they can recognize and respect. Someone as aggressive as they are." Her smile turned up a notch as she poked a finger in the middle of his chest. "Someone like *you.*"

"What!" He fell back a step.

Jenny laughed at his startled expression. At least she had his full attention now. He was no longer darting glances over his shoulder every few seconds. The man struck chords in her that she didn't know she had, but he was a bit on the uptight side sometimes.

"My coleader quit this morning," she told him. "I think you'd make a terrific replacement."

His deep blue eyes fairly popped out. "You're kidding, right?"

She shook her head. "Not at all. Poor Emily was the nervous type. She just couldn't cope with the kids. You aren't the nervous type, are you?"

He looked offended. "Certainly not."

"I didn't think you were. So will you take the job?"

"You're nuts. I can't be a Sunshine Girls leader."

"Why not?"

Carter stared. *Were her big brown eyes blind?* "I'm a man."

She treated him to a dazzling smile. "Yes, you certainly are. That isn't a problem, though. You can be the father figure that's missing in most of the girls' lives."

He gritted his teeth in frustration. "Now, wait just a minute. I don't want to be their father figure, uncle figure, brother figure, or cousin figure. The only figure I intend to be is a stranger figure."

"But Carter—"

"Forget it, lady."

She glared at him, losing that good-natured poise of hers. "Don't call me *lady* in that tone of voice. It sounds so awful." Her irritated expression smoothed out. "The name's Jenny. Remember, you've seen my underwear."

That reminder just about did him in. He either had to kiss her or get out of there fast. He chose the latter.

As he pivoted and strode through the doorway, he heard Jenny call his name. He kept moving.

"Tiffany!" His voice came out sharper than he'd intended. He saw his daughter start, then cast a wide-eyed look at him. He softened his tone. "We're going home now."

Tiffany came running.

"Don't make her go home," Lara cried, rushing up to him. "Please, Mr. Dalton. She wants to stay here."

She curled an arm around his daughter's waist as though he might snatch Tiffany away. "Tell him you want to stay," she begged Tiffany.

Carter watched the two girls exchange an anxious glance. A slow, wondering smile touched his lips. It seemed his friendless child was friendless no more.

He stooped down and caressed Tiffany's cheek with the tips of his fingers. "Do you want to stay?"

She hung her head. He decided it was just Lara whom she liked. Maybe she didn't want to hurt Lara's feelings by saying she didn't want to stay with the rest of the group.

"Lara can come to our house to play sometimes," he told her. "But I think it's best that we go home now."

"Please, please let her stay," Lara begged.

Standing beside Carter, Jenny hid a grin. She knew quite well that particular tone of voice of Lara's. It fairly vibrated with abject misery, the kind especially conducive to making an adult believe her whole world would collapse like soggy angel food cake if she didn't get her way.

Carter shook his head, though. "I'm sorry."

He did look sorry, Jenny thought. But she could see he was still determined he was right to take his child and run.

She took pity on him and came to his rescue. "Lara, Mr. Dalton has made his decision."

He shot her a grateful look. "I'm sorry this didn't work out."

"So am I."

Lara slipped over to her, and Jenny put her arm around her daughter's shoulders. Together they watched the Daltons leave.

He won't be back, Jenny thought with regret. And even though he'd mentioned getting their children together to play, she doubted it would happen.

The other girls came forward and gathered around her and Lara. Jenny's gaze traveled over their faces. They all seemed unusually contrite.

"We're sorry," JoJo said, acting as spokesman for the rest. "We didn't mean to scare those people off."

Heads bobbed in agreement.

JoJo pulled at the bill of her baseball cap. "We'll call Miz Smith and tell her we're sorry too."

Apparently, the word had spread about Emily quitting.

Jenny smiled. "I think that would be a nice thing to do."

Cheryl bumped up against Jenny's side and wiggled her way under her arm like a puppy demanding attention. "Do you think Miz Smith will come back if we promise to be real good?"

"Perhaps." She didn't have the heart to say that

she was reasonably certain Emily had decided to take a permanent vacation from volunteer work.

Cheryl clung to her. "You ain't leaving us, are you? I don't want you to ever go away, Miz Johnson. I like you a whole lot."

There were murmurs of agreement from the other girls. They moved in closer to Jenny, tightening the circle they made around her.

Jenny smiled at them one by one. She wished Carter could see this side of her girls; the sweet, affection-starved side that melted the adult heart and made the most rowdy behavior forgivable.

She hugged Cheryl. "I like you a whole lot, too, my little pumpkin pie. I like all of you. Let's sit in our friendship circle now."

A man can't raise a little girl by himself.

His mother's words echoed through Carter's mind that evening as he stood in the doorway of his daughter's bedroom. He couldn't blame her for saying it, for believing it when he had taken on so few responsibilities in the primary care of his daughter during the first seven years of her life.

He had been born the oldest of three sons to traditional parents whose opinions of male and female roles were sharply defined.

Sugar and Spice. Moms stayed home to rear the children.

Snails and puppy dog tails. Dads went out to make a living.

Antiquated as that seemed to him now, he'd fallen into line with those beliefs in his youth. He'd thought it was just the way things were supposed to be.

At twenty-four he'd stood at the altar and promised Carol forever. Lovely and sweet at twenty, Carol's background and life expectations had matched his.

The early years of their marriage had gone according to design. Carol had worked hard at being a wife and hostess. He'd worked hard at being a success and making a comfortable life for them. Tiffany had been born to schedule. Every Christmas card afterward had shown the beginnings of a perfect family.

When he was thirty-three Carol informed him that she didn't love him anymore. She wanted more out of life than carpools, PTA meetings, and dinner parties. Carol packed his bag. She got the house, the child, and a job as a minimum-wage receptionist. He moved into an apartment with furniture rented from Confused-About-To-Be-Divorced-Guys-R-Us.

Carol died in an automobile accident two years later. Her mother and his had both wanted custody of their granddaughter, each arguing they were better suited for the responsibility than he. But Carter had wanted the opportunity to make a secure and happy life for his only child. He knew he'd failed in many ways as a husband and father the first time around. This time, he couldn't afford to fail.

After months of watching Tiffany grow quieter, withdrawing into herself until she seemed nothing more than a sad little shadow, he'd made the decision to leave Jonesboro, the bedroom community of Atlanta where he'd been born and raised. He'd reasoned that he and Tiffany needed to distance themselves from the constant, though well-meaning, interference of his and Carol's families.

A man can't raise a little girl all by himself.

At times he feared his mother was right. This was one of those times. He didn't know beans from rocks about little girls. That morning's fiasco with the Sunshine Girls was a perfect example.

Carter rammed his fists into his jeans pockets, refusing to wallow in negative thoughts. He glanced around the pink, white, and gold room. Dolls, books, toys, and games were neatly arranged on shelves. Nothing was out of place. Everything looked organized and tidy.

His gaze came to rest upon Tiffany. Love swept through him like music that was at once sweet and painful to hear. In all his life he had never known anything as pure or as consuming as his love for his daughter.

Demurely clad in a pink nightgown, she sat very still on the cushioned window seat. With her porcelain skin, jet-black hair, and dark blue eyes, Tiffany did look like a fragile china doll that Lara had compared her to.

The kind for looking at. Not for playing with.

It occurred to him that something was wrong with that image. Just as there was something wrong with Tiffany's stillness, her silence, the neat perfection around her.

"Hey, Tiffy," he called out, trying to ignore the hard lump forming in his throat.

She looked up at him. The uncertain smile wavering on her rosebud mouth made the lump in his throat get bigger.

"I'm sorry about this morning." He crossed the room as he spoke and sat down on the bed's pristine counterpane.

She fixed him with a steady blue-eyed stare.

Carter locked his hands uselessly together between his knees. "I guess I made a mistake in taking you to the Sunshine Girls' meeting."

She turned her face to the window.

"I don't blame you for not wanting to stay."

"I wanted to stay." Her voice was so soft, he thought he hadn't heard her correctly at first.

"Did you say you *wanted* to stay?"

She nodded.

"Really?" Astonishment and confusion warred until he didn't know which was which. "You liked those girls?"

"Uh-huh." She clasped her small hands together. "They liked me too. I want to be a Sunshine Girl. Can I, Daddy? Please?"

Carter was speechless for a moment. His first inclination was to say no. But Tiffany hadn't asked him for anything since Carol had died. Not even a toy at Christmas. How could he deny her the one thing she asked of him now?

Her eyes were wide with wistfulness. "I'll be real good, if you'll let me."

"You're always good."

He got up and walked over to the window seat. Bending down on one knee, he kissed the top of his daughter's head, loving the feel of her silky hair. "All right, baby face. We'll try it and see how it works."

She smiled up at him.

Carter's heart melted. It had been a long time since he'd seen her cheeks grow rosy with pleasure.

FOUR

"I cannot believe you let Carter Dalton get away," Maureen said in disgust. "What's the matter with you?"

It was Sunday afternoon. Maureen had invited herself over, and she and Jenny were sitting in the kitchen drinking iced tea.

"Carter isn't a fish," Jenny said. "He's a man with a will of his own." She ran her finger around the edge of her glass. "Didn't we have this same conversation on the phone yesterday?"

Maureen looked as if she might rap Jenny's knuckles with a ruler. "Well, we're going to have it again. Up close and personal."

"I can hardly wait."

"Sarcasm is an unbecoming trait."

T-Beau flew over and buzzed Maureen's head. "Gaaaah! It's rude to come and spoil the fun."

"Go soak your head in a water dish," Maureen groused, smoothing her hair back into place.

T-Beau flew off to sit on the curtain rod. He stared down at Maureen and uttered little parrot sounds of dismay, a kind of whistling hoot. Jenny couldn't help grinning, for it was the kind of noise African grays made in the wild when their enemies were around.

"What did you really think of Carter Dalton?" Maureen asked.

"Oh, he seemed nice."

"*Nice* is a picnic in May. That puny little word doesn't do justice to a man like Dalton. You know what I want to know." Maureen cocked her head and smiled. "Did Carter melt your butter?"

Jenny conjured up a mental image of Carter Dalton—tall, broad shoulders, blue eyes to die for—and she wished he had elephant ears, a huge honker of a nose, or a downright mean disposition that would make him less than perfectly desirable.

She squirmed in her chair. "No, he did not. The man alphabetizes magazines," she added in a frustrated tone.

Maureen shook her head and gave Jenny a mock scowl. "The jerk! How dare he be so organized. And to think I was going to invite him to be your partner at my dinner party."

Jenny looked blank. "What dinner party?"

"You know, the one I'm giving Saturday night." Maureen averted her gaze. "Don't tell me you've forgotten."

"How could I forget something you never told me?"

"Mark and I are having a few friends and some of his business associates over for dinner. I'm certain I mentioned it to you before." Maureen still wouldn't look at her. A sure sign she was fibbing her pleated linen pants off.

"Bah humbug," Jenny said. "I'll bet you dreamed it up Friday afternoon when Carter Dalton walked into your classroom."

"Jennifer Kathleen! Have I ever lied to you?"

"Well, yes."

Maureen gave her an amused look. "Okay. Other than when I tell you I'm not going to introduce you to another man and then I do."

"Other than that, rarely," Jenny admitted.

"We've got to find you a man."

"No, we don't. If you want me to come to your party, I don't mind coming alone."

"*I* mind. I will not have my only sister be the odd woman out at my table. It's bad luck."

"Mo, when are you going to stop trying to find me a husband?"

Maureen grinned. "As soon as you make an effort to find one yourself."

"I appreciate your interest in my welfare, but would you cool it?"

Maureen bent down to pick up Miss Kitty, who was rubbing against her ankle. She cooed to the black cat, "Tell your mistress it isn't right for her not to have a dinner partner or a love life." To Jenny she said, "Don't you get tired of going to bed alone night after night?"

Jenny laughed as she shook a finger at her sister. "I knew you'd get around to the bedroom sooner or later, you little devil."

"Well, what do you do in bed to keep warm on a cold night?"

"I turn on the electric blanket."

"A warm body is more fun."

Strange sensations unfurled in Jenny as she wondered what it would be like to cuddle up to Carter's warm body on a cold night. She felt uneasy with the path her thoughts were traveling.

"Come on, Jen, invite Carter to my dinner party. You don't have to marry the guy. Just have some fun for a change."

"I barely know him," Jenny protested. "Besides, I don't think he wants anything to do with me."

Her sister picked up the portable phone on the table and held it out to her. "You won't know unless you ask. Call him."

"No." Jenny took the phone away from her.

"Chicken," Maureen taunted. "Cluck, cluck, cluck."

The phone rang as Jenny was trying to come up with an equally childish response. She answered, "Joe's Bar and Grill. Joe speaking."

"I'm sorry. I must have dialed the wrong number." The masculine voice was a rich, dark baritone. She knew that voice. Carter Dalton.

"That's okay," she squeaked in embarrassment. Before she could hit the disconnect button,

Carter said, "Jenny, I recognize your voice. Please don't hang up on me."

Busted. She felt her cheeks flaming.

"I can hear you breathing," he said. "Say something, Jenny." The husky tone of his voice produced gooseflesh on her skin.

"Hello, Carter."

"At last, she speaks." He sounded amused.

Maureen pinched her arm and whispered excitedly, "Invite him to my dinner party."

She glared at her sister and shook her head. Maureen sat back and pouted.

"Just out of curiosity, what's with the Joe's Bar and Grill business?" Carter asked.

"I get a lot of pesky telephone sales calls. It makes them think they've reached the wrong number."

"It's certainly a creative method to deal with unwanted callers." He paused. "Am I one of those unwanted callers, Jenny?" His voice had become low and seductive.

"Oh, no." That came out much too quick and breathless for comfort. Jenny steadied herself and asked casually, "What can I do for you?"

There was a longer pause, a faint laugh, then, "That's a loaded question. I've thought about that quite a bit lately. Hearing your phone voice gives me something else to think about."

She tried very hard not to let his sexy innuendo get to her. Still, it fired her imagination and made bothersome feelings come alive inside her.

"You have a 'feel good' voice," he went on. "It reminds me of a chocolate sundae—sweet and delicious."

Breath and heat lodged in her throat. If any other man had said that to her, she would have laughed it off and made some teasing remark. But with Carter, all she could do was wait for the heat to dissipate and for her breathing to return to normal. "You didn't answer my question, Carter."

"Ah, what can you do for me. For starters, you could forgive me."

"Okay, I forgive you. Why am I forgiving you?"

"I was rude to you and the Sunshine Girls yesterday."

"Oh, that. I do wish you and Tiffany had spent more time with the girls. They're nice kids. Really they are."

"I'm sure they are," he returned smoothly. "We need to talk, Jenny."

"Sure. Go ahead."

"I meant in person. Would it be inconvenient if I came to see you in about half an hour?"

The thought of him coming over made Jenny's heart work rapidly, like the sump pump in the basement during a heavy storm. It was nothing to get excited about, she told herself. He probably just wanted to apologize in person. Maybe he'd even reconsidered his decision about not allowing his daughter to join the Sunshine Girls.

"All right," she said finally. "You're welcome to come over."

"May I bring Tiffany with me? My house-keeper is out of town this weekend visiting her mother."

"Certainly. Lara will be glad to see her."

They traded good-byes and hung up.

Maureen let out a squeal of delight. Miss Kitty took exception to the noise and jumped down from her lap. "Carter Dalton is coming here?"

Jenny nodded absently, still caught up in the effect he had on her.

Maureen stood. "I'm going home. Be sure you invite him to my dinner party. Or else."

Jenny glanced up and frowned. "Or else what?"

"I'll tell Mom how your bedroom window screen really got broken when you were fifteen."

"That's blackmail!" she shouted at her sister's back.

Maureen smiled over her shoulder and gave a little Princess Di wave.

"You're here already!"

Carter scanned Jenny's flushed face. Why did she sound and look so surprised to see him and Tiffany at her door?

"Are we too early?" He glanced at his watch and saw that precisely thirty minutes had passed since he'd phoned her.

"Oh, no." She laughed and motioned them to come in. "That was a fast half hour, though."

He refrained from saying that the laws of time, like physics, always remained the same. Apparently, their awareness of time was quite different.

Jenny closed the door, then walked over to the stairs and shouted, "Lara, our guests are here."

She turned back to Tiffany and smiled brightly. As she chatted with his daughter, Carter studied her with a hungry, sweeping gaze. He hadn't been able to get her out of his mind. She'd constantly invaded his thoughts and his imagination since he'd met her.

She was wearing a loose T-shirt tucked into short cutoff jeans. The cutoffs showcased the beautiful expanse of her legs right down to her socks and tennis shoes. The fact that she hadn't bothered to dress up for him pleased rather than disappointed him. He chose to think it meant she was comfortable with herself and comfortable with letting him see her as she was.

He heard Tiffany's breath sucked in on a gasp of fright, and he tore his gaze away from Jenny's legs. His daughter's face was puckered in distress.

Carter wasn't too sure what happened next. He reached out his hand toward Tiffany and opened his mouth to speak. There was a rumbling bark behind him, then something large and furry pushed past him, almost knocking him off balance.

He'd just realized it was that damn Saint Bernard, when the thing pounced, driving Tiffany back against the door.

"Daddy!"

Carter swallowed a lump of fear. "Get him off her!" he shouted as he and Jenny both made a dive for the dog.

"Happy! Sit." Jenny grabbed the dog's collar and dragged him down.

Carter slid down to his knees and reached for his daughter. Tiffany hurled herself into his arms on a low wail. Her arms went around his neck in a stranglehold and she clung to him. She shook so hard, he could hear her teeth chattering.

He hugged her tightly, holding back through the sheer force of will a frightened spate of angry words. "Are you all right, Tiffy? He didn't hurt you, did he?"

Tiffany shook her head against his neck. "Scared me. I thought he was going to eat me."

"I know, honey, I know. It's all right." He buried his face in her hair.

"Carter, I'm so sorry."

His angry reprimand went unspoken as he glanced up and met Jenny's gaze. She looked almost as upset as he felt.

Lara came over and crouched down beside him. "Don't be afraid," she said, patting Tiffany's shoulder. "Happy just wanted to give you a kiss." She lifted anxious eyes to Carter. "He wouldn't hurt her. Honest, he wouldn't."

"Perhaps not," he said, controlling the tone of

his voice. "But she didn't know that. It's scary having a big dog jump on you."

Tiffany drew in a shuddering breath and raised her head. Her lower lip still trembled. Carter followed her gaze to the huge creature behind them and saw, thankfully, that Jenny still held on to his collar.

"A kiss?" Tiffany sounded half doubtful and half intrigued. "He gives kisses?"

Lara nodded. "Big, sloppy ones. Happy's a nice dog. He didn't mean to scare you. He just wanted to make friends with you. Hold out your hand and let him sniff your fingers."

Carter hugged his daughter more tightly against him. "I don't think . . ."

His voice trailed off as Tiffany lifted her arm and stretched out her hand. He looked around as the dog rubbed up against his back, tail switching, tongue lolling. Happy's goofy dog grin and expression gave the impression that he wondered what fun new game they were playing.

"Give Tiffany a kiss," Lara commanded her pet.

Carter held his breath as the dog nuzzled Tiffany's fingers with his nose, then he licked her, leaving a wet trail across the back of his daughter's hand.

Tiffany giggled. Relief flooded through Carter, followed by a buoyant feeling. It was good to hear her giggling.

"Yuck!" Tiffany giggled again as she wiped her

hand on her father's shirtsleeve. "Daddy, he likes me. He gave me a kiss."

Disaster averted, Jenny thought, watching the white-lipped tension drain from Carter's face. "Lara honey, put Happy out in the backyard. Then, if it's okay with Mr. Dalton, you and Tiffany can play in your room for a while."

Carter nodded permission. Tiffany scrambled away from him and went with Lara to let the dog out.

"I'm sorry," Jenny said again. "I put T-Beau in his cage because I could see he made you nervous the last time you were here. I wish I'd thought to put Happy out too. I would have if I'd known Tiffany was afraid of dogs."

"I don't think she's afraid of them, but she isn't accustomed to being around them."

He was silent for a moment, gazing at her with those remarkable deep blue eyes. "Jenny—" he started, then stopped and shook his head.

"What?"

He moved closer to her. "Every time I'm around you, my game plan goes out the window."

Her brow knitted. "Game plan?"

He accompanied his shrug with a husky laugh that made her yearn to hear it again. "Before I walked in the door, my thoughts were organized. I knew what I wanted to discuss with you and how long it would take. But being around you disrupts my thoughts, punches holes in my logic, and trashes any plan I come up with."

Jenny couldn't help feeling mildly annoyed that he'd come to see her with a plan and a timetable. "Maybe you need to loosen up, Carter. Life doesn't always go according to plan. Some things are beyond our control." And no one knew that better than she.

"That's true," he said softly. "I didn't plan to let you get under my skin."

There was that darn word again: *plan.* What might have been a thrilling declaration of attraction turned into a backhanded and confused message.

He didn't seem to notice her annoyance. His smile was slow and devastatingly sensual. "But you do get to me, Jenny Johnson. You do."

A flood of excitement washed away her annoyance. "You . . ." She'd meant to tell him not to say things like that, not to look at her that way. But the words got lost and she felt too light-headed to think straight.

She nervously clasped her hands together. "I don't understand you at all." What she didn't understand was herself and why *he* turned her knees to water when other men couldn't.

"That's okay," he said in a voice even softer than before. "I can't figure you out either. And I like it."

His smile grew wider and his eyes darkened. He lifted his hand to cup her chin, tilting her face up to his, and she knew he was going to kiss her.

Some things are beyond our control.

Jenny hadn't known when she'd said that to him that this would be one of those things. She remained perfectly still, her eyes fluttering closed. Anticipation filled her, anticipation of tasting the sensuality of his lips.

In her twenty-nine years of living, she'd experienced the gamut of first kisses, from hunt-and-peck to conquering barbarian. But this . . . this first kiss with Carter was the way first kisses should be. Unhurried. Full of sweetness and the promise of greater things to come. Thrilling right down to the toes.

A first kiss should create a need for more. When Carter lifted his mouth a fraction from hers, Jenny felt the frustration of many unfulfilled needs.

"Silk," he murmured, sliding his fingers through her hair. He brushed his mouth across hers and drew back again. "And flames. I knew it would be that way with you."

She swayed closer to him, keeping her balance by placing her palms against his chest. She could feel the steady beat of his heart beneath her hand, could hear the echo of her own heartbeat in her ears.

Need for the promise inherent in those first sweet kisses drove her to seek more. Her lips moved over his, then parted in invitation. He responded with an urgency that shook her. She moaned softly and moved her arms up to circle his neck.

Passion—the kind she'd read about in romance

novels and in women's magazines, the kind she'd always daydreamed about but never quite believed existed—left her dazed and breathless.

Where was all this sensuality inside herself coming from? Had it been waiting all along? Waiting for the right man to ignite it? Or was it simply a matter of perfect timing? She was a woman raising a child alone. Lonelier for that warm body next to hers in bed than she'd ever dared admit to her sister . . . or to herself.

The sounds of a door slamming and of running feet had them quickly breaking apart.

"The kids," Jenny said, still submerged in the discovery of a part of herself she hadn't known existed.

"The kids," he repeated, looking as bemused as she felt.

"Hi-bye," Lara called out gaily. She rushed past them with Tiffany close on her heels.

Jenny drew a deep breath, her gaze still locked with Carter's as the girls disappeared up the stairs.

Carter closed his eyes and shook his head. "I think life just got more complicated."

She agreed wholeheartedly. If Mr. Structure and Objectives was her Mr. Right, then heaven help them both. She had a terrible feeling no two people on earth could be more ill-suited for each other than she and Carter Dalton.

❖———————❖

Burger King was crowded. Balancing a heavily loaded tray, Carter followed Jenny and the two girls to a vacant booth by the window that looked out on the enclosed playground. Tiffany and Lara slid in on the same side, leaving him to share the other seat with Jenny.

An hour ago, he'd kissed Jenny. And he was still rattled. He thought about that while he distributed burgers and drinks.

Kissing her was something he hadn't planned on, even though he'd thought about it quite a bit since Friday afternoon. He hadn't planned for a simple kiss to knock him for a loop, either, but it had and then some.

He'd gone to Jenny's house intending to spend a pleasant few minutes making polite conversation. To apologize for overreacting on Saturday and to accept her challenge to colead the Sunshine Girls so he could keep a watchful eye on his daughter. That was it. An hour tops spent in her company, then he and Tiffany would say good-bye.

Instead, he'd had his life turned upside down. He'd kissed her! To prolong his reason for being around her, he'd sat on her sofa and let her *coax* him into agreeing to colead her motley crew. Then the invitation for her and Lara to join him and Tiffany for dinner had come out of his mouth before he'd given the matter any thought at all.

And here they were. Looking like a family unit out for a quickie dinner on a Sunday evening.

Giggles drew his attention to the girls as he

lifted a packet of fries. Lara's ash-blond head was bent close to Tiffany's as she whispered something in her ear. The dulcet sound of Tiffany's giggles delighted him so much, he didn't move, merely gazed at her animated face.

It had been too long since he'd seen his daughter react so spontaneously. Even if he hadn't already found Lara as irresistible a pixie as her mother, this talent she had for making Tiffany laugh and come alive would endear Lara to him forever.

"Are you holding those fries hostage," Jenny asked, "or are you going to let us have some too?"

The girls giggled again.

"I was thinking I might have to eat them all myself," he teased. "I'm sure these girls don't like french fries."

"Daddy! Yes, we do."

"We love french fries, Mr. Dalton."

Jenny chimed in, "Try to withhold a single fry and the three of us will wrestle you to the floor."

"And we'll tickle you 'til you beg for mercy," Lara said, shaking a finger at him.

Jenny nodded, her eyes sparkling with laughter. "I promise you, it will be a horror-frying experience."

"Electro-frying," Tiffany said solemnly. She and Jenny traded a glance and dissolved in giggles.

"Oh, no," Carter groaned, seeing the delight on both their faces at having discovered a mutual love for bad puns. "No puns, no tickling. I give up! Fries for everybody."

During the meal, Carter discovered that Lara could eat and talk at the same time and, surprisingly, that Tiffany knew as many knock-knock jokes as Jenny. Their voices and laughter flowed over him, smooth and steady. It didn't matter what they were saying. It simply felt good to listen to the happy sound of their voices and their laughter.

Warmed from within, Carter didn't think to object when the girls begged to go out to the playground. He did turn to watch them out the window. "Do you think we ought to go out with them?" he asked Jenny. "That slide looks high to me. What if—?"

"Don't borrow trouble," Jenny cut in.

He met her gaze. "They could get hurt."

She leaned forward and put her chin on her hands. "Or they could have a great time without scraping so much as a knee."

He frowned. "You aren't concerned?"

"No. We can see them from here." She smiled. "Relax. The kids will have more fun if we're not standing over them, watching everything they do."

"You think I'm being overly anxious?"

"Just a little."

He thought about that for a moment, then he glanced out the window again. Tiffany and Lara were splashing around in a sea of colorful balls. A red one flew up and hit Tiffany on the head. He winced, wondering if that had hurt. Apparently it hadn't, for she burst out laughing, and with her hands sent a shower of red, yellow, and blue raining down on herself and her friend.

"I guess they'll be okay." He turned back to see Jenny smiling as she watched the children play. "It's remarkable," he added, shooting another quick look at his daughter.

"What's remarkable?"

"The change in Tiffany. I haven't seen her so animated, so talkative in—" He shook his head. "Maybe it sounds silly, but I feel like a parent whose sick child has been miraculously cured."

"It doesn't sound silly at all." She smiled at him, and in her gaze he saw a full measure of the deep compassion Mrs. Robbins had told him about. A silent understanding passed between them, and he knew nothing else needed to be said.

Carter found himself doing as she'd suggested. He let go of his worries and relaxed. It was easy to do that around Jenny. She was a special lady. Sensitive and cheerful, she was a delight and a total mystery. In her presence, there were no shadows in his child's eyes. And when she kissed him, he burned.

Desire wasn't all he felt for Jenny, he admitted to himself. He liked her. Perhaps too much.

"Would you like some coffee?" he asked. It was an inane thing to say, given the way he was feeling at the moment. He ought to be thanking her for making his little girl laugh again. But he had a feeling she would only shrug it off. Laughter was something that came as naturally to Jenny as breathing.

She nodded. "Yes, thank you. With cream and fake sugar."

Light and sweet, he mused. Just like Jenny. He smiled at his own absurdity.

Jenny couldn't take her eyes off Carter as he slid out of the booth and made his way toward the front of the restaurant. As good as he looked in a business suit, he looked even better in jeans. He had long runner's legs, and she liked the way the denim stretched across his thighs. She found that observation vaguely disturbing.

She realized with a jolt that every time she was with Carter, the sexual tension grew stronger between them. She felt breathless and anxious and exhilarated all at the same time.

She didn't want to feel so strongly attracted to him, she reminded herself desperately. But she could not ignore it. Just being around him made her feel alive and womanly in a way she'd never felt before.

She stared out the window for a long, contemplative moment. If the next few weeks of being around him were going to be like this, she was in for big trouble.

"Hi ya, babe."

Jenny looked up. Hank Flowers, the Lothario of the YMCA Nautilus set, stood beside the booth. He was a pain in the drain sometimes, but a harmless one. She managed a smile.

As Carter wound his way back through the crowd, he paused when he saw a man talking to Jenny. His gaze traveled over the guy. Mid-thirties, sun-streaked hair, muscles honed from hours regularly spent pumping iron. A homeboy, he judged by the few friendly waves and several calls of "Yo, Hank, how's it going?"

Carter formed an instant dislike for him. Why, he wasn't sure. Maybe it was the proprietary way the man looked at Jenny. Maybe it was the overly familiar manner in which he touched her shoulder.

Who was Homeboy Hank to Jenny? Was he her ex-husband? Carter hadn't spared the ex a thought before. Now he wondered about Mr. Johnson. Was he still involved with her and their child? If so, was that good or bad? Did he make Jenny unhappy?

The heat of the coffee penetrated through the cups to his palms. It was an uncomfortable feeling. As uncomfortable as the jealousy rising up like a newly awakened and quite vicious beast.

That thought shook him. Carter had never considered himself a jealous person. What the devil was wrong with him?

His gaze fell upon Jenny. Hot memories of how she had burned in his arms exploded again in his head. She was sweet and passionate.

Undisciplined, too good-natured, too messy, his logical side countered. *Don't get personally involved*. He had a new business to get off the ground, a child to raise, and no time to waste on a woman.

If you didn't want to get involved, why'd you kiss her?

Because I couldn't resist, stupid.

Even as he debated with himself, he noticed that for once Jenny's open, friendly face held a closed expression. She wasn't enjoying the man's attention. That realization gave him a disgusting jolt of satisfaction.

Ex-husband or casual acquaintance, Jenny looked like she needed help getting rid of a pest. A gentleman would definitely come to her rescue.

Carter drew in a breath and plastered a smile on his face. *Watch out, Homeboy Hank,* the jealousy beast in him said. *You're history.*

FIVE

Jenny half listened to Hank as she patiently waited for him to wind down his standard "go out with me" spiel. Interrupting him was no good. She'd tried it before, only to have him start over again from the beginning.

Hank Flowers was firm muscles, golden male beauty, conceit, vanity. But, God bless him, he was a bit on the dense side in the brains department.

"I'll show you a good time," she heard him say. He always finished with that line. Every time he said it, Jenny couldn't help mentally picturing the two of them standing in front of a glass-encased exhibit entitled: *A Good Time*.

"I'm sure you could, but—"

"Here you go, darling."

Jenny gaped at Carter. *Darling?* she repeated to herself, watching as he reached past Hank to set a cup on the table in front of her.

"I'm sorry it took so long, darling." The expression in Carter's blue eyes was at odds with the warm smile upon his mouth. If she didn't know better, she'd think he was jealous that she was talking to Hank.

No, she thought. He couldn't be jealous. It was too high schoolish.

He turned his head and stared Hank up and down. "Is this man bothering you?"

What in the world had gotten into him? she wondered. Carter looked as though he'd toss Hank through the window, if she asked him to.

"Now see here," Hank sputtered. He glanced at Jenny, clearly confused. She didn't blame him, since she'd told him dozens of times that she didn't date. And here was Carter, calling her *darling* and acting like a jealous lover.

Men were just plain weird, she decided. They were both looking at her as though she was a territory they each had their eye on conquering.

She quickly introduced the two men, throwing in that Hank's grandfather had founded the YMCA where she taught aerobics and that Carter had recently moved to the city from Atlanta. She had to bite her tongue to keep from adding, "You have something in common: You're both men and you're both weird."

Hank eyed Carter with new interest. "So you're from hot 'Lanta. Man, I love that happening place. Bet you find our little town boring."

"Not at all," Carter said, looking at her instead

of Hank. "Greensboro is a city that hasn't lost its small-town warmth and friendliness. In fact, I'm just beginning to discover how charming it can be." The smile he aimed at her was slow and very intimate.

She felt hot color bathe her cheeks. She ignored that along with the swift racing of her heart.

Hank glanced from her to Carter. "Are you two like dating or something?"

"No," she answered quickly.

Carter didn't contradict her. He just kept smiling.

Lord love a duck, she thought. Things were getting out of hand.

Slightly exasperated, she said, "You guys ought to get together sometime. Pump iron, play racquetball." Let 'em play their boy games over something besides her.

"Say, that's a great idea." Hank brightened at the suggestion. Ten to one, Jenny thought, he was envisioning himself kicking butt on the racquetball court. "Give me a call. Jenny has my number."

Carter gave him an amused look. "I'm sure she does. It's a pleasure to meet you, Mr. Flowers. I'd ask you to join us, but Jenny and I have a great deal to discuss."

"Hey, no problem." He moved aside, then winked at Jenny. "See ya at the Y, babe."

As Hank left and Carter slid onto the seat beside her, she gave an exasperated sigh. "Carter

Dalton, would you mind telling me what that was all about?"

"You needed rescuing."

"I didn't need rescuing."

"You looked like you did."

"Well, I didn't."

He gave her a skeptical glance. His eyes were so very blue in the artificial light, she thought. She drew a deep breath, fighting the lassitude invading her bones.

"I can take care of myself. Really, I'm not the helpless type," she added quickly, more for her own benefit than his. It was a little reminder to herself that Jenny Johnson didn't get all warm and mushy inside over a man.

She felt herself turning pink. Warm and mushy was exactly how he made her feel. Rats, cats, and bats, she cursed inwardly.

Carter noticed the blush staining her cheeks. "I didn't mean to imply that you couldn't handle yourself."

"Yes, you did. People tend to think small women are as vulnerable as children. If I were taller, you'd probably think I could handle anything."

A smile tugged at his mouth. "If you were six feet tall, my reaction would have been the same."

"Ha!"

"It's true. You didn't look happy when I saw Hank talking to you. I thought he was bothering you. In fact, I wondered if he was your ex-husband."

"You did?" She burst out laughing. "What an appalling thought!"

"Does he live in Greensboro?"

"Who? My ex-husband?"

He nodded.

"No. Greg doesn't live in Greensboro." For a moment she looked as though she would leave it at that. Then she said, "We lived in Durham when we were married. I came here after the divorce to be near my family. Greg's in Colorado now, teaching philosophy at a college out there."

Dozens of nosey questions raced through Carter's mind. Before he voiced any, he glanced out the window to check on Tiffany and Lara. They were safe and they looked like they were having a great time. Just as Jenny had predicted. He smiled to himself, glad for the chance to sit and talk with her a bit longer.

He returned his gaze to Jenny and launched the first question. "Are you still in love with your ex-husband?"

Jenny caught the interest in his voice and felt a quick lurch in her middle. "Why do you want to know that?"

He leaned back, stretching his long legs out, and watched her intently. "I'm curious about you, that's all. You said you don't date. I wondered if it was because of him."

She looked down, toying with her cup. "I have

a lot of reasons for not dating. What happened with Greg is one of them."

"What happened?"

"He couldn't keep his hands off the coeds." There, she'd said it aloud. She waited for the residue of hurt to follow. It didn't. There was no pain. Not even a hint of the weary shame she'd once felt.

"He had affairs with his students?" Carter sounded appalled. "What a bastard."

She lifted her head and met his gaze. He looked solemn, his eyes somber. "I thought so too at the time. Now, it's just kind of embarrassing." It was true, she thought in amazement. No hurt, no shame, nothing but a buzz of discomfiture.

His gaze drifted to her mouth, then back up to meet her eyes. "Jenny, you don't have anything to be embarrassed about."

The tenderness in his voice startled her. She fought off the warm, tingling stirrings inside her. The booth seemed too confined suddenly, and Carter too disturbingly near. Sunlight fell across his handsome face, highlighting the angles and lean bone structure.

He was so beautiful, she thought with a rising ache in her throat. She'd sworn she'd never allow herself to be attracted to another man who was prettier than she. Her heart began to pound, and she had to look away, out the window. She watched their daughters play for a long moment, hoping her stomach would stop jumping, her heart would settle down.

The frightening truth was that she was enthralled with Carter Dalton.

Mr. Beautiful. Mr. Structure and Objectives.

Was she a glutton for punishment or what? Why couldn't he be pug ugly and happy-go-lucky?

His voice broke into her thoughts. "Jenny, I'm sorry if talking about . . . him upsets you."

"He no longer has the power to upset me." Saying it aloud felt good. She turned her head to look at Carter. His warm smile encouraged her to risk opening up a bit more. "Do you want to know why I married Greg?"

"If you want to tell me." He brushed her hand with the backs of his fingers. His touch made her smile.

"I was nineteen, a very young and immature nineteen, when we met at UNC at Chapel Hill." She laughed self-consciously, visualizing herself at that age and finding the image painful. "I didn't have the slightest idea of what I wanted to do with my life. My parents were teachers. Maureen had just started her first teaching job. For lack of interest in anything else, I declared myself a physical education major, and eventually did get my degree.

"Greg was so different from me. He knew exactly what he wanted and how he was going to get it. I was so impressed that everything he did was well planned and orderly. I saw him as someone who could give my haphazard life order and purpose. I think he was attracted to me because of my relaxed, unconcerned attitude. And of course, that's the first thing he wanted to change about me."

She laughed again and shook her head, her hair drifting around her face like a cloud. "Why do people do that? Try to change the people they love, I mean."

"A quirk of human nature, I suppose," Carter said. He lowered his gaze to her mouth. He couldn't help it. Her lips were lush and tempting, and madly enough, he wanted to kiss her again.

"I did try," she said softly, as though speaking not to him but to herself.

"Try what?" He raised his gaze and wondered why he'd ever thought her plain. She was beautiful and oddly dangerous. Dangerous because she brought out a man's instincts to protect and cherish.

"Try to change," she answered. "I was so eager to please back then that I tried to be everything Greg wanted me to be. I kept our house spit-and-polish clean, wore prim suits to faculty teas, and shopped at Laura Ashley for mother-daughter dresses. For years, I was so busy being Greg's ideal professor's wife that I didn't realize what a little robot I was turning into. And a blind one at that. I was the last to know about his affairs."

She shrugged and laughed again. She was a survivor, Carter thought admiringly. A willow that could be bowed by the pressure of a fierce wind, but couldn't be broken. His esteem for her rose another notch.

He caught and held her gaze. "He was an idiot. A selfish man like that doesn't deserve someone like you . . . and Lara."

Her eyes widened in surprise. For a long moment, she stared at him, then a smile played about the corners of her mouth. The smile grew. It was like watching spring awaken.

Carter responded to it like a flower desperately needing the sunshine. He lifted his hand to caress her cheek. "Don't let one bad experience keep you from dating again, Jenny. You deserve to be happy."

She turned her head and brushed a kiss on his palm, surprising him. He felt a sweet flash of desire, and he wanted her more than he'd ever wanted any woman. It shook him, and confused him, that he could feel so intensely about her. They were opposites—she open, exuberant, easygoing, and he reserved, intense, controlled.

"I am happy," she said, her breath warming his palm. "You're a nice man, Carter Dalton. I think it will be good having you for a friend."

The dewy touch of her lips remained long after she had pulled away.

Later that evening, Carter wandered out onto the deck that ran the back length of his house. He slouched down in a chair and rested his heels on the railing.

He felt unusually restless. His concentration—

legendary among his peers in his profession—was shot. He'd walked away from a pile of work on the kitchen table. The time and motion study he'd been trying to work on held no interest for him.

Glancing around in the twilight, he felt more aware of spring's awakening than he ever had before. It was in the greening of the trees. It was a scent in the air.

Spring's awakening. He remembered Jenny's smile, the feathery kiss she had brushed onto his palm, and her scent of flowers and female.

He looked up at the darkening sky. The first line of a poem he'd had to learn in high school came back to him.

Jenny kissed me.

The poem hadn't made much of an impression on him in his youth. It had been another one of those silly things English teachers made students read and memorize.

Jenny kissed me.

Tonight, he understood the poem. It confused him to feel so . . . unlike himself.

"Damn the woman," he muttered. Confusion was not on his list of approved states to be in.

Stay away from her. That's what he'd do.

Then he remembered that keeping his distance would be difficult. He was committed to spending every Saturday morning with her until school was out.

Carter stared straight ahead, fists rammed into his pockets, his muscles tensed. "Damn," he muttered again. It was going to be damn hard to keep Jenny Johnson in a box marked "impersonal" for five long weeks.

Friends. She wanted to be friends. Okay, he could handle that. Friends they would be. That was as personal as he would allow himself to get.

Tuesday afternoon, Jenny literally ran into Carter on the sidewalk in front of their daughters' elementary school. She was walking backward, looking at her sister, and trying to hear what Maureen was calling out to her above the noise of the children streaming around her.

"What?" Jenny shouted as she barreled smack into an adult-size person. Two hands caught her arms.

"Sorry." She glanced up and back. "Oh, it's you."

"Hello, Jenny." Carter gave her a crooked half smile and released her.

She turned, unconsciously rubbing her arms where his touch still burned. Though he'd stepped back, she could feel the imprint of his body on hers.

He stared at her. She stared back, heart pounding. They measured each other across the short distance, and the air hummed with an undefined tension. Carter's eyes gleamed with unbanked fires. He had never looked at her with such heat in his gaze, even when he'd kissed her Sunday. His gaze took a slow tour down her body, lingering on her breasts, which tingled with awareness. When he brought his eyes back to her face, they were filled momentarily with desire and a faint reluctance. The school yard seemed, suddenly, too small and too crowded. Without a touch, a word, or a sound, she felt intimately connected to him.

"Hi, Mrs. Johnson."

Tiffany's voice broke the spell. Jenny drew in a shaky but grateful breath, and she smiled down at the child clutching Carter's hand. "Hi there, Miss Tiffy. Did you have a good day at school?"

"Yes, ma'am. We learned to count to ten in Spanish." Her dress was so perfectly white, with tiny pearl buttons. A white band with a pretty silk rose held back her shining black hair.

"That's terrific." She leaned down and hugged the fairy princess, because she looked like she could use one.

Tiffany offered her a shy smile, and Jenny's heart turned over. Maybe it was just the mother in her responding to a child that needed mothering, she thought, but it was impossible not to fall in love with this little girl.

She raised her gaze to Carter. His expression was now as unreadable to her as a Chinese newspaper. Maybe she'd only imagined the heat and desire in his eyes. She shook off a disturbing disappointment.

"So, how are you?" she said brightly. It was lame, but she couldn't think of anything else to say.

"I've had better days." He let out a tense sigh, running his hand over the back of his neck.

"Having a bad day?"

He nodded. "My housekeeper usually picks Tiffany up from school and takes care of her until I get home from work. Mrs. McGee quit without notice this morning, because she needs to care for her mother who is seriously ill. I understand her circumstance, but not having any time to make other arrangements sure puts me in a bind."

Jenny murmured sympathetically. "I know that's a disaster situation for a working single parent."

"It certainly is. I've been running from one meeting to another all day, so I haven't been able to research after-school care for Tiffany."

"What are you going to do?" She eyed the little girl with concern.

"Take her to the office with me. I've got a four o'clock meeting." He frowned and glanced at his watch. "I'll be tied up for the rest of the day with that. But my secretary can keep an eye on Tiffany while I'm gone."

"That sounds awfully boring for this cutie pie," Jenny said. "Why not let her come home with me and Lara?" She smiled at Tiffany. "Would you like that?"

Tiffany nodded. "May I? Please, Daddy?"

Calm, controlled, unruffled. Carter had told himself he'd exhibit those qualities the next time he saw Jenny. He was none of those things, thanks to the bewitching woman.

He stared over her head for a moment, collecting his thoughts—not an easy project with her so temptingly near. A reliable baby-sitter and a real home setting for his daughter was infinitely preferable to leaving her with his secretary at the office. But if he let Tiffany go home with them, he'd have to see Jenny again after work. Not smart, given how she affected him.

The logical part of his mind told him to decline her offer. Another part—the one concerned with the welfare of his daughter, or so he rationalized— jumped at the chance.

He found himself saying, "Are you sure having another child in the house won't disrupt your schedule?"

She grinned. "Lara and I do have a full calendar this afternoon." She winked at Tiffany and began ticking off items on her fingers. "We have to walk the dogs, water the flowers, watch cartoons, play in the backyard." She paused and looked thoughtful. "Or was that walk the flowers and water the dogs?"

Tiffany laughed.

"Okay, okay." He gave her a grateful smile. "I guess that was a silly question. Thank you, Jenny."

He took her hand in his. It was a casual gesture, a friend greeting a friend, but he was aware of unnerving physical sensations from the brief touch.

"You're welcome."

"I appreciate your help," he said, releasing her hand. "I'll come for Tiffany about six o'clock."

"That will be fine."

Touching her had been a mistake, he thought dismally. How could he possibly hope to keep his relationship with her confined to friendship, when merely touching her hand sent hot lust rushing through his veins?

He tore his gaze from her and searched the inner pocket of his suit jacket for one of his business cards. "If you need to get in touch"—he frowned at the word *touch* and the images it conjured up in his mind—"with me before then, call my office and leave word with my secretary."

"Okay." The tips of her fingers met his as she took the card from him. She drew her hand back almost as quickly as he did.

She looked at him so warily, he wondered if she had felt the same sensation he had. For that instant their fingertips had touched, he'd experienced something not unlike shooting sparks.

Carter mentally sighed and chucked plan *A* out the window. Thinking he could keep his relationship with her under tight control was ludicrous. Plan *B* began forming in his mind.

He tried to keep his voice steady as he rattled off the name of Tiffany's pediatrician. "Maybe I'd better write her doctor's phone number on the back of my card," he said, groping in his inner pocket again for a pen.

"Don't bother. I can look it up in the phone

book." Jenny shoved the card into the pocket of her jeans, drawing his attention to her hips. A woman in tight blue jeans had never been a turn-on for him before. He swallowed hard. Until now. For a skinny little thing, Jenny filled out a pair of jeans like nobody's business.

"Don't worry about Tiffany, Carter. I'll take good care of her."

He nodded.

Jenny held out her hand, and Tiffany slipped hers into it. "Let's go find Lara. Do you like chocolate cake?" she asked as they started to walk away. "Last night we made the best chocolate cake. When we get home, we'll have a great big piece—"

"No cake," Carter interrupted.

They both turned and looked back at him. It was a toss-up to say who was frowning the hardest.

"No sweets after school," he said. "That's the rule at our house."

"Well, shoot." Jenny looked as disappointed as his daughter. "What can she eat?"

"Fruit. Peanut butter and crackers. Anything healthy." He might not know beans about raising a girl alone, but seeing to it that Tiffany's diet consisted of nutritious foods was one thing he could do.

Jenny murmured something that sounded like "Party pooper." Then she said to Tiffany, "I guess we'll have to cook up something healthy. How do you feel about brussels sprouts?"

"Yuck."

She laughed. "Don't worry, sweetie, I was just teasing."

Carter lightly touched her arm, reclaiming her attention. "Tiffany has to do her homework before she's allowed to play or watch television."

Jenny acknowledged that with a salute. "No junk food, no playing and no television before homework."

"Right."

"Boy, is your father tough," she said to Tiffany as they started off again.

His daughter nodded. "Do you really take your flowers for a walk?"

"Of course! I have a pot of begonias that just love a nice walk on a sunny day."

The sound of Tiffany's giggles remained with Carter until he'd almost reached his car. Then he found himself wondering what he was going to do about Jenny.

He did not want to be affected by her, but he was. She was impulsive and generous. Life loving. Full of laughter and fun. She made him burn with a mere touch of her fingers. There was no getting around it. He wanted her. He did not want to want her, though.

What a hell of a mess.

The only thing to do was to date her until the fire burned out.

Unfortunately, there was a stumbling block in the way of that plan.

Jenny didn't date.

She liked him, though. Carter was sure of that. He thought of the way she'd responded to his kiss at her house, the way she'd later pressed her lips to his palm.

Jenny kissed me.

He felt a sweat break out on his brow, felt a tightening in his loins. Oh yes, the attraction was mutual, but neither of them were saying anything about it.

Clearly, she wasn't interested in a serious relationship. Neither was he. A serious relationship required more time and attention than he had to give.

Casual dating he could handle, though. He was human enough to want a little female companionship. It would be heaven to have a warm body next to his in bed sometimes—with no strings attached, no promises of anything more.

His first plan of action would be to find a way to change Jenny's mind about dating. He was working on that when a stray thought stopped him in midstride.

Jenny had said something about taking the dogs for a walk.

Dogs?

Surely she'd meant *dog*.

His heart sank. Knowing Jenny, he wouldn't be surprised to discover she'd acquired another mutt since Sunday.

Carter decided he had lost his grip on reality. Why else would he be planning to get intimately involved with a woman who had a child and her own petting zoo; a woman who gave her dog a teddy bear for a mistress, took flowers for walks, and voluntarily spent her Saturdays with a bunch of wild, unruly children?

As he got into his car and drove away, Carter knew he'd just been fooling himself. Involvement with Jenny would be far from friendship, far from casual dating. He was already more emotionally involved with her than he wanted to be—and he was far from liking it.

Jenny was searching the living room for library books—they were two weeks overdue, according to the notice she'd gotten in the mail—when she heard Tiffany say her name. She glanced over her shoulder. Tiffany stood behind her, cradling Boo to her chest as though the fat gray cat were a doll.

"Hi, sweetie. Are you finished with your homework?"

"Yes, ma'am."

Boo squirmed. Tiffany set him down, and he ran under a chair.

"I was just wondering . . ." The little girl lowered her gaze and scrubbed at the floor with the toe of one pink tennis shoe. "Daddy's not here yet. Do you think he's okay? He's supposed to pick me up at five."

Jenny glanced at her watch and saw that it was

twenty minutes after the hour. "He's just a little bit late. I'm sure he'll be here soon."

Tiffany didn't look up. "But what if he's dead?"

"Oh, sweetie." Jenny reached for Tiffany's hands and drew the child down on the sofa. "Why would you think that?"

"My mom was supposed to pick me up from school one day. But she had a car accident, and she died."

She stared up at Jenny, looking small and defenseless, her eyes shadowed with a weary kind of fear at odds with her age. It made Jenny's heart ache. Girls of eight were supposed to be filled with laughter and the carefree joy of simply being alive.

She smiled at Tiffany and drew her close. "I'm sure your daddy is fine. His business meeting might have taken longer than he thought. He could even be tied up in traffic. He'll be here soon."

The child seemed to relax, and after a few minutes of cuddling against Jenny, she ran off to play with Lara.

SIX

"She actually asked if you thought I was dead?" Carter dropped down in a chair and braced his arms on the kitchen table.

"Yes." Jenny opened a cupboard and took out a bottle of aspirins.

He swore softly and rubbed his aching temples.

"Stop obsessing about it," she said with quiet firmness as she filled a glass with water. "Tiffany was worried and needed a little reassurance, that's all. Next time you're going to be late, give the kid a phone call."

"The situation is more complicated than remembering to call home," he said testily.

"No, it isn't," she said just as testily, setting the pain relievers and water glass down in front of him. "You're just ticked because you didn't think of it first."

Carter had his mouth open for an irate reply

when he caught himself. "Thanks," he muttered, reaching for the aspirins. As he chased the tablets with water, he stared at her. Her eyes held his, sweet and rich and deep enough to drown in. He let his gaze run slowly over her, and he marveled again at how tiny she was next to him.

"The first year can be rough," she said softly. "Lara and I had some tough times after the divorce. But we got through it. So will you and Tiffany."

He gazed at her thoughtfully. It wasn't any of his business, but he wanted to know. "Does Lara's father keep in touch with her?"

The light went out in Jenny's eyes. "No, they were never close. She hasn't seen Greg in over a year." For a moment, her lower lip trembled, then she got it under control.

As if she'd revealed too much in that simple statement, she stood and whisked the glass off the table. As she washed it out at the sink, T-Beau swooped down from the curtain rod where he had been hovering like a small, beady-eyed vulture. The parrot perched on her shoulder and rubbed his beak against her ear as though he knew his mistress needed comforting.

Carter swore silently, wishing he'd kept his big mouth shut. She had taken his daughter into her home, had comforted her when she needed it. In return he had raked up past hurts and made Jenny stop smiling. Not a fair exchange.

"Lara took Greg's disinterest hard for a while,"

she said, still facing away from him. "Then she just seemed to accept it. The Sunshine group helped, I think. One day I heard her telling Sarah that some people weren't born reliable, like her dad, and that you had to accept people for what they were."

Carter shook his head. "That's a hell of a thing for a child to have to learn so young."

She turned toward him, the parrot still perched on her shoulder. "It told me, though, that Lara had sorted through her feelings about her father and had come up with an answer she could live with." She paused, then added in a softer tone, "You can adapt to anything, I guess."

She picked up a spongy orange ball from the counter and tossed it onto the floor. T-Beau cried, "Braaak!" and swooped down to pounce on the ball.

Turning, Jenny looked out the window above the sink. "Early evening was always my favorite time of day. A time of peace and contentment and . . . hope. For a while after . . . the divorce, it became the loneliest, saddest time because I could not feel those things. I used to cry in the early evenings. Then the wells dried up and I stopped crying for good. I had adapted. The peace, the contentment, the hope came back. And you know, I don't take those feelings for granted because I know what it's like to live without them."

Her simple words touched Carter deeply, all the more so because she'd spoken in a manner that did not ask for sympathy. *That was how it was then; this is how it is now.* No more. No less.

Impulse led him to get up and walk over to her. Once he stood near her, he had second thoughts about giving her an impulsive hug. He knew that once he touched her, she would feel too damn good between his hands.

She turned gracefully and faced him. "How's your headache?"

"Almost gone."

She looked her usual serene self, arms folded, eyes full of normal curiosity.

Some hot, tight emotion swam up in his chest, squeezing his heart. The timing sucked, but he badly wanted to ask her out.

How still her face was for a moment, he mused, as though she struggled with some internal question. Then her expression became emphatic. The dark thick lashes surrounding her eyes fluttered once, her soft mouth, so eloquent of kindness, stretched into a smile.

An unmistakable Jenny smile. That great warm smile fired the beauty molded in her face. Could a heart stop beating and the man still live?

"My sister is having a dinner party Saturday night," she said. "Maureen's been bugging me to invite someone to be my dinner partner. Would you like to go with me?"

The question caught him off guard. It was as though the tip of a hot wire touched a nerve in his body.

"You're inviting me to dinner?"

Jenny saw the astonishment on Carter's face. She managed a laugh, even though her heart felt small and tight in her chest.

"You say that as if I just asked you to hand over your wallet."

"I didn't mean to sound . . ." His voice trailed off. He began again. "You surprised me, that's all."

Jenny was more than a little surprised herself. Amazing, she thought, that as hard as it had been for her to issue the invitation, it was even harder for her to await his response.

Maybe he wouldn't accept. Maybe he would. Maybe he'd think the invitation meant more than it did. She'd gone out with men before who thought a dinner or a movie entitled them to a roll in the hay. She took a deep breath, steadying herself, forcing an outward calm she didn't feel inside. What would she do if . . .

If, if, if. Maybe, maybe, maybe.

What good did it do, worrying about ifs and maybes? What good did it do, worrying and making plans, and more plans, if the first plans failed? It was futile worrying about every decision, worrying about every day. It was impossible to know what was coming.

Leaning back against the cabinet, Carter watched her. Jenny had thrown him an unexpected curve by asking *him* out. His plan to wear down her resistance was unnecessary, he thought with some irony.

"I thought you didn't date," he said.

"Oh, I don't. It wouldn't be a date. I tried dating a few times. But the men turned out to be boring or slimy." She smiled suddenly. "Present company excluded."

"At least until I bore you or do something slimy?"

She blushed as prettily as a sunset.

"Doesn't taking you to your sister's dinner party count as a date?"

"Oh, no," she said with a shake of her head. "I'd go by myself, but Maureen thinks it's bad luck to have an unequal number of men and women at her table."

Jenny looked completely at ease as she stood with one hand braced on the countertop. Only when her fingers drummed against the butcher block did Carter realize she was nervous.

"You wouldn't even have to pick me up," she went on. "We could meet at Maureen's house. That way you won't have to stay, if you're not having a good time."

Carter held her gaze in silence for a long moment. He reinstated his plan to wear down her resistance. Dinner at her sister's house was as good a place as any to start.

Finally, he said, "All right."

"You will?" She looked surprised, and he realized she really hadn't expected him to agree.

He smiled to himself. "Certainly. A nondate

sounds interesting. What time should we meet Saturday?"

"Time!" T-Beau screeched as he rolled on the floor with the spongy ball. "He's murdering the time!"

"Nobody's talking to you, silly bird," Jenny said, laughing. "Seven o'clock, Carter. I'll give you directions to Maureen's house before you leave."

She lowered her gaze and smiled with delight. "Oh, you're awake!"

"What?" Carter followed her gaze, and he saw that her smile wasn't for him.

At his feet was a puppy of indeterminable parentage. It had a long body, stubby legs, and a mushed-in face. It was covered in sleek golden fur, overlaid with a faint saddle of longer black hairs.

"You did get another dog," he said with disbelief.

"Uh-huh. Isn't he a cutie? I rescued him from a neighbor who was going to take him and his three littermates to the pound. I found homes for all of them except this little guy."

He warily eyed the odd-looking creature. It was sniffing his left shoe. "You aren't going to keep it, are you?" he asked hopefully.

"Of course. Lara and I adore him. She named him Rags."

"Don't you already have enough pets?" His gaze darted from the puppy, to the parrot, to the numerous feeding dishes lined up against the wall near the door, and back to her.

"There's always room for one more. Pets," she informed him cheerfully, "are excellent for teaching a child responsibility."

Carter didn't disagree, but he thought *one* pet would be sufficient.

"Oh dear!" Hot color flooded her face.

He followed her gaze down to the floor again and almost had a heart attack.

The mutt was peeing on his left shoe.

He let out a yell and hopped from one foot to the other.

"No! Bad dog." Jenny snatched the creature up in her arms.

"Bad, bad, bad," T-Beau echoed, circling around the room. He swooped over and landed on Carter's shoulder as Jenny rushed out the back door with the mutt.

Carter stood very still, not knowing what to do or what the bird was going to do to him. Slowly he inched his head around to look at T-Beau.

The parrot stared at him. Then he said, "Damn dog."

Carter laughed. "You got that right, buddy." He relaxed and experimentally raised one finger to touch the bird's horny, reptilian toes. T-Beau's claws were sharp, he thought, sharp enough to prick skin. It amazed him how gently the parrot clung to his shoulder.

T-Beau stayed with him as he cleaned off his shoe and the surrounding area of the floor. When Carter washed his hands, T-Beau hopped down on the countertop and peered into the sink. He made a noise that sounded like, "Wishhh-shh, gurp-gurple," and Carter wondered if he was imitating the sound of the water going down the drain.

"You really are smart, aren't you?" He ran his hand over the bird's back the way he'd seen Jenny do.

The back door opened and closed. Jenny came in without the dog.

"I'm so sorry." Her color was high as her eyes searched his face. She launched into rapid speech as she walked over to him. "It takes a while to housebreak a puppy. Are you mad? I wouldn't blame you, if you were. You don't like animals very much, do you? I—"

"Jenny," he said, interrupting the flow of words. "You're right. I'm not overly fond of animals."

She sighed. "I was afraid of that."

"I am, however, becoming rather fond of you." He drew a finger down her cheek. "And since you have a houseful of critters, I'll tolerate them. Given enough time, I might even learn to like them."

The simple act of touching her aroused and warmed him. He knew she saw the desire in his eyes, because breath caught in her throat. It irritated him that she took a step back.

"That's nice. I like you too." She hesitated, then smiled nervously. "I think we're going to be good friends, don't you?"

She was still denying the attraction between

them, he thought, and he didn't like that. He wanted her more than he had ever wanted a woman before. He wanted to go to her now, taste the fragrance of her silky skin, fill his palms with her small, firm breasts. He wanted to experience every part of her inside and out.

And she only wanted to be friends.

Damn. His desire for her left him open to being vulnerable in a way he had never been. He didn't do vulnerable well.

Patience, he counseled himself. If he pushed too hard too soon, he'd lose the new objective he'd set his mind on: getting Jenny into his bed.

"Yes," he said finally, "I think we're going to be very good friends."

Jenny was uncomfortably aware of Carter staring at her and she tried to ignore the tension coiling in her stomach. Some of what she was feeling must have shown, though, for an amused expression crossed his face.

He smiled at her, a wonderful deep, warm smile.

She took another step back, her gaze roving over the room, trying not to let that smile get to her or to let her knees buckle. "Oh my goodness!" she exclaimed, catching sight of the time on the wall clock. "It's later than I thought. I forgot all about dinner. I'm famished. I bet the girls are too. Would you and Tiffany like to stay for dinner? It won't be much. Just soup and sandwiches."

"Sounds good to me. I'm starving. What can I do to help?"

Stay out of my way. Don't smile at me. Don't touch me.

Jenny berated herself for being so silly. He was a new friend, a guest in her home. That's all. "Take off your jacket and tie."

His eyebrows shot up. Her smile faltered, for she saw a flicker of sexual intensity in his vivid blue eyes.

"Roll up your shirtsleeves," she went on, striving to infuse lightness in her voice. "Kick back and relax. You've had a rough day."

"As you wish." He crossed to the table, then turned to face her as he stripped off his jacket and neatly draped it over a chair. Impeccable as always, he was wearing an immaculate white shirt, crisp and fresh against his skin.

Mesmerized, Jenny allowed her gaze to drift over his wide shoulders, his powerful forearms where he rolled up his shirtsleeves, and his broad, long-fingered hands that reached up to loosen his necktie.

A slow, sensual smile crossed his handsome face as he held her gaze. She felt a lurch in her chest and squelched it. She had only meant to encourage him to make himself at home and be comfortable. Instead he'd performed a little striptease that made her want to move nearer to him, to feel the warmth of the masculine heat that drew her. Lost in her yearnings, she jumped when he spoke.

"I didn't have time to check into after-school care for Tiffany."

She watched his mouth as he spoke, remembering those warm lips covering her own, and she shivered.

"She likes being here with you and Lara."

Until she exhaled, she didn't know she had been holding her breath. "We like having her with us."

He kept smiling. His eyes flickered over her body, and her skin tingled with awareness. His gaze returned to her face, and she could only return the hypnotizing stare of the piercing eyes that cut deep into her soul.

"Would you consider," he went on, his voice husky, "keeping her after school until I find another housekeeper?"

She swallowed hard. Her hand went to her throat, where her pulse beat jackhammer fast under her fingertips. "I'd like that. So would Lara. She's decided Tiffany is her new best friend." Her laugh sounded breathless and intimate. She hadn't meant it to sound that way. "I must admit, Tiffany's wormed her way into my heart."

"I don't know how long it will take to find a suitable housekeeper. I'm very particular."

"It doesn't matter. I'll keep her as long as it takes."

He exhaled heavily. "For as long as it takes," he repeated. "I was hoping you'd say that."

She saw his gaze dip to her breasts. The nipples

responded, hardening to prominent points under her thin cotton T-shirt.

As he met her gaze once more, she felt tension simmer between them, a tension that had nothing to do with what they were discussing. Seductive sexual heat electrified the air, arousing turbulent sensations in her. The situation would have been laughable, she thought, if she were watching this happen to someone else. But it wasn't laughable. It was thrilling, frightening.

She wasn't sure she liked what was happening. Nor was she certain she liked the excitement that surged through her at the flash of possessive desire she saw in his eyes.

Confused, and more than a little mortified by her body's response, she turned away. "How 'bout a glass of iced tea? I love iced tea. With lots of ice," she babbled. Lots of ice. Maybe she ought to bathe her traitorous body in a shower of ice.

"Yes, thank you." Carter pulled out a chair and sat down. He felt everything in him grow tight as he watched her walk from the refrigerator to a cabinet. Her movements were graceful, beautiful, and in that instant all he could picture was her stretched out beneath him on crisp sheets, a floor, any surface would do. He wanted her fiercely, desperately, almost obsessively.

He cursed to himself and shook off the insistent, throbbing need. Already he'd let her get too close. He'd have to proceed carefully, if he was to keep his heart detached.

When she cast a spooked glance at him over her shoulder, he resolved to keep himself under firmer control. T-Beau flew over and perched on his shoulder, distracting him for a moment.

"T-Beau! No," Jenny called out, starting toward the table.

"It's all right," Carter said. "He isn't bothering me." The parrot rubbed his beak against his ear. "Why is he doing that?"

Jenny smiled. "It's a sign of affection. You should be flattered. T-Beau's quite fussy about who he likes."

He returned her smile, relieved that the tension had seeped out of the room. Wanting to keep things calm, he chose the first subject that came to mind. "Tell me about the activities you have planned for the Sunshine Girls for the next five weeks."

"I haven't planned beyond this Saturday." She threw a quick grin at him. "Like I told you, I kind of fly by the seat of my pants from one meeting to the next."

"No plans?" He frowned in disapproval. "Jenny, don't you know anything about running an organization? Even an informal one needs some structure, discipline, objectives. What are the girls supposed to do this Saturday?" He paused, then added with a mocking grin, "Besides create mayhem and havoc, that is."

Jenny's chin went up. She kept her cool with

some effort. "If you don't like the way I lead the group, maybe you should take over."

"Okay."

"Fire safety," she said, walking over and handing him a glass of iced tea. "That's the topic for this week. Several of the girls are latchkey kids. I want to make sure they, as well as the others, know what to do in the event of a fire in the home. Think you can handle that, champ?"

"I'll manage," he said, smooth as silk. "Fire safety is an excellent topic. I'll study up on it. By the way, would you answer a question?"

"Depends on the question." She moved back to the refrigerator and took out a head of lettuce and a large plastic container of homemade vegetable soup.

"Last Saturday, I saw that chubby little girl—"

"Cheryl." Jenny hauled a large saucepan out of a cabinet.

"Okay, I saw Cheryl picking something out of your hair . . ." his voice trailed off, then strengthened, "and eating it."

"It was raisins," she said, as though having them in one's hair was as normal as shampooing.

"From the food fight."

She glanced up from ladling soup into the pan. He was frowning. The food fight had really offended his sense of decorum. Tough. "That's right, from the food fight."

"I'm not going to ask why you let them get

away with that. But why did you allow what's-her-name to eat raisins from your hair?"

It annoyed her that he'd forgotten the child's name. More than any of the girls, Cheryl needed to be remembered. She needed love and affection. She needed to feel she was important to someone.

She glowered at Carter as she broke off a leaf of lettuce for T-Beau. The parrot swooped over and grasped it in one claw, then flew off to the far side of the kitchen to gobble down his treat.

"What's-her-name is Cheryl," Jenny said, exasperated. "Please try to remember that. And for your information, no one who values their life gets between Cheryl and food."

Carter gazed at her questioningly. "Has a problem, does she?"

She placed the full saucepan on the stove and turned on the heat. "I told you before, all of them have problems. Some worse than others." She looked at him and sighed. "You didn't believe me, did you?"

"I do now." Carter no longer had any trouble believing a couple of them had been kicked out of the Girl Scouts. "Would you mind if I took over planning and scheduling activities for the group?"

She eyed him skeptically for a second. "All right, if you really want to. Do keep in mind, though, that we function as a support group. The girls need a say in what activities they want to do, because they have so little control of the other things happening in their lives."

That made sense to him. Still, he thought Jenny gave the children too much power, and that's why they ran all over her. "Okay. I'll come up with a list of suggested activities, and we'll go over it with them on Saturday."

She nodded, but gave him a warning glance. "Don't try to pack too many activities into one day. The girls need unstructured time for having fun and talking to each other. We have a friendship circle at each meeting. Sometimes they have so much to say that I end up tossing the day's planned activity out the window. That's one of the reasons I don't get too hung up on planning. Sometimes it's more important to just go with the flow."

It sounded like a haphazard approach to him, though Carter refrained from saying so. Children responded to structure and discipline. He'd show Jenny how effective planning and organizing could be. He'd show her how smoothly the group could move from one activity to another without the mayhem and havoc.

"We have four meetings after this week," he said, thinking aloud. "Five or six ideas ought to do it."

"Seven meetings."

He looked up as she crossed the kitchen and opened a door that revealed a walk-in pantry. "Seven? I thought the group stopped meeting at the end of the school year."

"We do. I'd like to take them on a special outing once a month through the summer. That way the girls can stay in touch and we won't lose our momentum as a group." She beamed a bright smile at him as she came out of the pantry with a loaf of bread and a box of crackers.

He eyed her uneasily. "Do you have anything in mind for these special outings?"

"I thought it would be fun to take them to Caro-Winds for the first one. It's an amusement park like Six Flags Over Georgia."

"I've heard of it. It's near Charlotte, isn't it?"

"Uh-huh. It's a blast. The girls will love it."

They probably would, but he wasn't so sure it would be a blast being cooped up in a car with those hellions on the two-and-a-half-hour drive from Greensboro to Charlotte.

Carter kept silent for a few minutes, alternately watching T-Beau roll on the floor with the spongy ball and watching Jenny prepare the meal. It suddenly struck him how much walking she was doing, and he glanced around, really seeing the kitchen for the first time.

It was long and wide, bright and plain. Everything looked old and scrubbed. One wall was covered with wooden cupboards and butcher-block counters. The refrigerator was at one end of the room, the sink in the middle, and the stove on the far end.

"This kitchen is incredible," he said. "I've never seen one so large."

Jenny glanced at Carter. He sat without moving, staring at her with an odd expression. "Thank you. I love big kitchens."

"You have to do a lot of walking in here."

"I've never thought about it, but I guess I do."

"In fact, you waste a lot of time going from one place to another. The refrigerator, sink, and stove are too far apart. Going from one to the other—not to mention the detours along the way for cookware, utensils, and ingredients—is like walking around the block." He shook his head. "It's organized wrong."

"It is not!"

"Yes, it is." His eyes narrowed in concentration as his gaze darted around the room, measuring, assessing. She knew she was seeing the efficiency expert in him rear its beastly head.

"Think function, convenience, and space," he said, rising from his chair. "You need to consider how you most use your kitchen. Are you primarily a baker? If so, creating a baking center where all ingredients and appliances are within easy reach should be a specific goal."

She made a short, derisive noise. "I like everything just as it is."

"Items should be stored close to where they are used," he went on as though he hadn't heard her speak. He walked over to the cabinet where she kept her pots and pans. Opening it, he hunkered down, and peered inside. "A rack suspended from the ceiling can provide an attractive and more functional way to hang your pots and pans."

Who was he to tell her where her pots and pans should go? It was her house, her kitchen, her pots and pans. "I like them fine just where they are," she said.

"Too inconvenient." He crossed the room and removed a small notebook and pen from his suit jacket.

"What are you doing?" she asked as he began scribbling in the notebook.

"Making notes. You really need a work island too."

The man was salivating for the chance to get his efficient hands on her kitchen! No way. She wouldn't stand for it.

"Carter, I don't want a work island. I don't want—"

"You need one." He smiled as he passed by her.

Jenny set her teeth. "Don't tell me what I need."

"It's my job to know what you need," he said, opening a cabinet and making a note of the contents.

Horrified, she rushed over and nudged him aside. She shut the cabinet, keeping her hand on the door. "No, it isn't your job. I haven't hired you to make my kitchen more efficient or productive."

He grinned. "Give me a dollar and you've hired yourself the best organizational development consultant in Greensboro."

"Forget it."

"Come on, Jenny." He hooked a finger over a brass drawer pull. "Work with me here."

"Not a chance."

He peeked into the drawer. "It'll be fun."

"In a pig's eye, it will!" She glared at him as he wrote something else in his notebook. "What are you writing now?"

"Just making a note that you store your flatware too far away from the dishwasher." When he moved on to the next drawer, she reached out and put her hand over his.

"No," she said, glowering up at him. "I don't want to be organized. I don't need to be organized."

He abruptly snaked an arm around her waist, pulled her close, and kissed her.

Her cry of startled surprise was quickly muffled. She didn't resist as he deepened the kiss. Instead, her arms inched up around his neck, and she clung to him as if he were preventing her from drowning.

Just when she was trembling with intoxicating need, he lifted his head and gazed into her eyes. "Jenny," he said with a smile, "I've never met a woman who needs organizing more than you."

She could have screamed in frustration.

SEVEN

Jenny picked the girls up after school the next day. After Tiffany climbed into the backseat of the minivan with Lara, she handed Jenny an envelope from Carter. Too curious to wait until later, Jenny opened it. Inside were four single-spaced typewritten pages.

Carter was uncompromisingly strict about his daughter's diet, she thought, scanning the first page. Three meals a day, two light snacks. Vegetables, fruits, whole grains, wheat bread only, pasta, fish, chicken, one serving of red meat per week, skim milk, frozen yogurt instead of ice cream, minimal salt, minimal sugar, minimal fat, no fun. Junk food and trips to fast-food restaurants fell in the category of rare special treats.

The man was a demon rulemaker.

The second page contained rules for grooming, dressing, studying, deportment in various social situations, a strict schedule of suitable television programs Tiffany was allowed to view, and activities Carter deemed appropriate for a child her age.

Good Lord! Make that an obsessive-compulsive demon rulemaker.

The third page was a detailed medical history, and the fourth a letter granting Jenny permission to seek emergency medical care for Tiffany if needed.

She stuffed the pages back into the envelope and sat staring out the windshield. She thought about Carter's list of instructions, thought about the man himself, and she wondered what she was getting into.

The answer was TROUBLE in big, fat capital letters.

The trouble was she liked Carter. Okay, it was more than like. She'd hardly stopped thinking about him since she'd met him. Strange sensations came over her when she was with him. He made her feel breathless with anticipation. Something existed between them. She couldn't deny it. However, she was afraid to count on it, afraid she was being presumptuous.

The trouble was that she and Carter were so different. She'd known right from the start that he was a man who liked order and structure. He alphabetized magazines and organized other people's kitchens.

But this—she tapped the envelope against the steering wheel—this was the stuff neurotics were made of. Was he truly a person of such rigid standards? Or was he just a scared single parent, going overboard in an effort to cope with raising a child alone?

Either way, Jenny pitied him and his daughter.

Once upon a time, she'd lived with strict guidelines for every occasion. Rules for conduct, rules for everything from how to clean the oven to what to wear for grocery shopping on Monday morning.

Eventually, the universal law that life was messy and unpredictable had caught up with her. Greg's affairs had woken her up to the realization that she had become a Stepford wife, a robot of a woman with no original thoughts of her own, living in an antiseptic world devoid of self-esteem and spontaneous joy.

The experience itself hadn't been a nightmare while it was happening. Waking up to it had been the nightmare, a profoundly shocking one.

She'd come a long way from being that programmed robot woman. She was unchained now, free to be the unique person she was, not to mimic what someone else thought she should be.

These days common sense dictated what rules she followed. Never stick anything smaller than a football in one's ear. Don't talk to strangers. Say the magic words please and thank you. Treat others as you wish to be treated. Do your best and you'll never be sorry. If a child begs for attention while you're washing the dishes, forget the dishes. Chores can wait, kids shouldn't have to.

Laughter welled up in her throat. It felt dark and helpless, and for a moment she feared it was going to turn into tears for Carter, for Tiffany, for the robot woman she used to be, for the part of her that went weak and mushy whenever Carter touched her.

She and Carter had so little in common, and it was foolish to think otherwise. He was perfection in an expensive business suit. She was a mess in worn denim. He was a planner. She let things happen.

Thinking in terms of a romantic relationship between them was not only presumptuous, it was impossible.

Jenny started the engine, reminding herself that she didn't want a man in her life anyway. Men expected things. Unreasonable things like a woman changing herself to please them.

Still lecturing herself, she drove to the YMCA. By the time she ushered the children through the wide glass doors into the lobby, she was convinced she was an idiot. A couple of kisses didn't mean Carter was interested in having a relationship with her. She was obviously beating herself up for nothing.

Lara tugged on her arm. "Mom, can Tiffany take gymnastic lessons with me?"

"If she wants to," Jenny answered absently.

It didn't occur to her until she was halfway through her step aerobics routine that gymnastics wasn't on Carter's list of approved activities. When she told him she'd let Tiffany sign up for the class, would he have a cow?

He was a demon rulemaker. He'd probably have a whole herd of cows.

That thought caused her to stumble on a diagonal slide step across the bench.

The children were so excited, they nearly tackled Carter when he came through the door at 6:15 that evening. Even Happy greeted him with all the fervor of an animal that has been denied human companionship for an unbearably long time.

Laughing, Carter pushed the dog away and went down on one knee to put an arm around each girl. "If I had known I'd get this kind of reception, I'd have been here hours ago."

"Daddy, I had the most fun day ever!"

"You did?" He kissed his daughter's cheek. When he felt Lara slip her arm around his neck, he instinctively turned his head and kissed her cheek too. She beamed a smile at him.

"Daddy!" Tiffany patted his face. "We went to the Y, and Lara let me wear her leotard and tights. Look at me." She squirmed away from him and pivoted on her toes like a ballerina.

Carter dutifully inspected the red leotard and white tights. She did look cute in her borrowed outfit, but it was the light in Tiffany's eyes and the flush of excitement on her face that made him smile. "Very pretty, baby face. It was nice of Lara to let you wear her clothes."

"Me and Tiffany are twins now," Lara said. "We decided it, and we're going to be best friends and sisters forever and ever."

He turned his head to glance at Lara and found her watching him with an expression akin to hero worship. Carter swallowed hard. What was it about this child that touched him so much? It wasn't just because she looked so much like her mother. There was something sweet and endearing about Lara, something that made him want to take care of her, that made him wish this lively little sprite was his daughter too.

Tiffany scrambled back into his embrace, reclaiming his attention. "I took gymnastics with Lara today. When we got home, Rags threw up in the kitchen. It was gross!" She giggled.

"Gymnastics? Who gave you permission to do that?" He jerked his head to one side as Happy licked him on the ear.

"Jenny. I can't do a back walkover like Lara yet. But Miss Julie says I'm a natural, and it won't be long before I catch up with the rest of the class if I practice a lot. Isn't that great?"

"Terrific," he answered, forcing a smile. "Lara, where is your mother?"

"Out on the deck."

He tucked each girl under his arms and stood up. Delighted, the kids squealed and laughed as he carried them through the house.

Carter didn't laugh with them. He was too busy imagining his hands wrapped around Jenny's throat.

"Gymnastics?" Carter bellowed, pacing the deck. "Are you out of your mind? It's dangerous. Tiffany could get hurt! She could break an arm or her neck." He streamed past, and Jenny quickly sidestepped in lieu of being mowed down.

"Anything can be dangerous." She threw up her hands in frustration. "I swear, you anticipate trouble more than anybody I've ever met."

"I do not." He gave her a steely-eyed glance. "I calculate the risks involved."

She wanted to take him by the shoulders and shake him. "Same difference. Jeez, Carter, with that kind of attitude I'm surprised you get out of bed every morning."

"We're not talking about *me*! We're talking about a fragile little girl!"

"Could you yell a little louder? I'm not sure the neighbors on the next street heard you clearly."

"I'm not—" he modified his voice, "yelling." He jerked at the knot in his tie until it hung loosely around his neck.

Jenny let out an exasperated sigh. "Let's get reasonable. I work at the YMCA three afternoons a week. Lara goes with me and takes gymnastic lessons. We love having Tiffany with us, but we can't completely rearrange our lives to suit you. So that leaves us with three options. One, Tiffany can stay in the nursery with the babies and toddlers. Two, she can sit on the sidelines, watching me lead a bunch of adults through a step aerobic routine, or she can watch Lara and the kids her age having fun in the gymnastic class. Three, she can join the class, learn something new, and have fun too."

She paused, waiting for him to respond. When he remained silent, she pressed on. "If I were Tiffany, I'd hate options one and two. Being stuck with the babies would be embarrassing. Watching the adults would be boring. Watching the other kids have fun would be even worse." She crossed her arms and looked him straight in the eye. "But she's your daughter. Tell me what you want me to do with her."

The fire went out of him. He dropped his gaze, and she realized his need to keep his only child safe from imagined dangers was at war with the influence of her perspective.

"Carter, did you participate in sports when you were Tiffany's age?" she asked, pressing her small advantage.

He glanced up, frowning. "Of course. But that was different. I was a . . ." His voice trailed off. He turned his back on her and braced his hands on the deck railing.

"A boy?" she finished for him. "Carter, I get the feeling you're stuck in another century. The one where boys were encouraged to reach for the stars, and girls were encouraged to reach no higher than a pantry shelf."

He remained silent.

She walked over and lightly shook his arm. "Wake up, boyo. We're fast approaching the year two thousand. Things have changed. Females of all ages participate in sports. They are doctors, lawyers, Indian chiefs, wives and mothers, truck drivers, politicians, and anything else they blooming well please."

"You've made your point." His voice had never been cold before. Never as cold and flat as it was now. "I grew up with two brothers, no sisters. You don't have to tell me I don't know a damn thing about what little girls do or don't do. I've heard it before. There, I've said it. Gloat all you want."

Her anger drained away as she began to understand where his attitude was coming from. He was a pawn to past conditioning. Carter had probably been raised to view females as delicate creatures in need of sheltering and protecting.

She placed her hand over his. "I'm not gloating. I'd never do that."

"I know you wouldn't." He continued to stare straight ahead. She had a feeling he wasn't seeing the azalea shrubs loaded with buds or the swing set and wooden jungle gym that occupied a corner of the fenced-in yard. His vision was turned inward, and she couldn't begin to guess what he saw there.

"You're too honest for petty emotion," he said,

surprising her. He turned his hand palm-up beneath hers and gave her hand a squeeze.

Carter felt her fingers close around his hand. It felt good, companionable, and it made it easier for him to open up a little. "I know I tend to be overprotective. I don't mean to look for danger in every situation, but I guess I do."

"I'll bet your mom believed in the 'you'll poke your eye out' school of thought," she teased.

He nodded, then said in a perfect mimic of his mother's voice, "Carter, don't run with a pencil in your hand. You'll fall and poke your eye out."

Jenny laughed. "I heard similar variations of that theme a million times when I was growing up. That and, 'Jennifer Kathleen, why can't you learn to be a lady like your sister?' "

"Jennifer Kathleen. That's pretty. I like it." He exhaled slowly and met her gaze. "A pretty name for a pretty lady."

"I'll tell my mother you said that. She won't believe the lady part, but she'll be pleased."

Her dark eyes were warm and stunning against the fairness of her skin. She looked like a teenager in an oversize black sweater and white leggings, with her hair in disarray and her face scrubbed clean. She really was beautiful with that sprinkling of freckles across her nose.

Pretty is as pretty does. That old adage was meant for Jenny. She had pretty ways that made her beautiful. She genuinely cared about other people.

Cared enough to speak the truth to a stubborn fool like him.

She smiled at him, her eyes shining. A spark arced between them, and he felt a surge of heat through his body.

"I'm sorry I yelled at you." He raised one hand and brushed his thumb over her cheek, adding teasingly, "It's wrong to raise one's voice to a charming pixie. She might cast a spell on the unfortunate lout."

Jenny laughed. "Is that how you see me?"

He nodded.

"I like the charming part. But a pixie?" She rolled her eyes. "I think there's a short joke in there somewhere."

"Not at all." He cupped her chin and tilted her face up to his. "Pixies are fey little creatures with the courage of giants."

"I'm going to take that as a compliment." She smiled. "I didn't mind you yelling. It's kind of fun arguing with you. Greg never would argue with me. He—" She broke off, blushing.

"Go on," he urged. "Don't be embarrassed to mention him. He's a part of your past, like Carol is a part of mine."

Her smile grew. Carter wished it wasn't so radiant, so candid. How easily she could lure him under. A smile. A touch. Something so simple shouldn't feel so complex, so overwhelming.

"Greg wouldn't argue or fight with me," she said. "He would get distant and philosophic. I hated that. It made me feel I was too insignificant to him for it to be worth his effort."

Encouraged by her openness, he said, "Carol and I didn't fight either. We swept our differences under the rug and pretended not to notice how crowded it was under there."

"I know what you mean," she admitted. "It's an awful feeling. Little problems go unresolved and grow into major ones."

She stared up at him. A moment of silence passed, then she said, "I owe you an apology. I didn't think before letting Tiffany join the gymnastics class. If you don't want her to do it, I'll take the heat, since it's my fault. I'll talk to her and explain things."

Carter recalled the excited light in his daughter's eyes when she'd met him at the door in her borrowed outfit. He shook his head. "No, it's a done deal. She seems happy about it, and I can't take that away from her."

"I promise I won't do anything like that again without discussing it with you first." She rose up on her toes and kissed his jaw. "You're a good man, Carter Dalton. I do wish you weren't so guarded, though."

"What do you mean by guarded?" he asked, running his thumbnail over her velvety palm.

"You guard yourself as closely as you guard your daughter. There are so many things I don't know about you."

"What do you want to know?" He slowly untwined his fingers from hers, not trusting himself to maintain the contact any longer.

She leaned back against the railing, looking up at him from beneath dark lashes. "I want to know what you were like as a kid. Who your best friend was when you were ten. I want to know what you like to do on rainy Sunday afternoons. Do you prefer the mountains or the beach? Did the rug finally get too lumpy? Is that why you and your wife split up?"

He took a deep breath. "I was a regular kid. I was the oldest, so I picked on Cam, my middle brother. Cam picked on Mike, our youngest brother. And of course, I'd give Cam more hell for picking on Mikey."

Jenny laughed. "Ah, the pecking order of siblings. Do you all get along now?"

"Amazingly well. My best friend from first grade through high school was Randy Griffin. He was the best pitcher Jonesboro High ever had. Baseball was our life."

"Rainy Sundays," she prompted.

"Tiffany and I rent movies and stuff ourselves with popcorn. I prefer the mountains." He grinned. "I don't like getting sand in my pants."

"And the lumpy rug?"

Carter felt something tighten in his chest. "That's a bit more complicated to explain. Perhaps I should save that sorry story for another time."

"Come on, champ. I spilled my guts to you in a Burger King booth. My backyard is a heck of a lot more private than a fast-food restaurant. There's no one here but you and me and Miss Kitty."

"Miss Kitty?"

She pointed to the black cat curled up on the bottom step of the deck. "Miss Kitty won't blab your secrets."

He couldn't help smiling. "It's payback time, huh?"

"You bet."

Maybe it was time, he thought, time he told somebody about that episode in his life. "Carol and I were the perfect couple. Everybody said so. Our backgrounds were similar, our values and expectations were the same. We were happy, at least I thought we were. Carol took care of the house, the budget, and the baby. I worked long hours and became a vice president of the consulting company I worked for. Things started changing after Carol miscarried our second baby. It was the first time something in our marriage hadn't gone according to design. We never talked about it. Life just went on as though the miscarriage never happened. I knew something was changing between us, but I didn't understand what it was or what to do about it. One day I came home from a business trip—I traveled quite a bit back then—and Carol told me she didn't love me anymore. She'd packed my bags and had them waiting for me in the hall closet."

"That must have been so painful," Jenny whispered.

"It was final, that's all." He shrugged dismissively, as though to say it was over and done with. But she wondered. Oh, how she wondered.

He averted his gaze, and she knew it was time to change the subject. "How was your day?" she asked lightly.

"Good." He met her gaze and smiled. "I caught myself looking out the window of my office and thinking about you today." He lifted a forefinger to trace one of her brows.

She struggled in a war of desire and resistance. She didn't know how to make room for them both, and the resistance drained away. "I thought about you too," she whispered.

He took a step closer, bracing his hands on either side of her on the deck railing. "I want to kiss you."

His gaze was like a warm caress. Jenny shuddered. He was so close, she could feel his warm breath on her face, feel his wonderful heat.

Go with the flow, Jenny girl, her inner voice whispered.

"I'd like that, Carter," she said simply.

It was all the encouragement he seemed to need. His mouth was like velvet, warm and smooth, as he kissed her. He lifted his hands and ran them through her hair. She wished he would move them over every inch of her that throbbed and ached with need.

He wanted her. She could taste the desire every time his lips met hers. She could picture soft music, candlelight, and a big, wide bed with the two of them tangled together. The image made her blush, heated her skin, and her mouth became more aggressive.

How long? she wondered dizzily. How long had it been since she'd been kissed so thoroughly by a man whose very touch made her heart pound? How long had it been since she'd responded to a man's kiss with joyful abandon?

Too long. Much too long.

A floodgate had been opened, and Jenny allowed herself to be swept along with the rushing currents of desire. She savored the erotic entanglement of tongue and breath and want and need. Her arms slipped around his neck, and she moved her tongue against his in sinuous, silken swirls. His fingers drifted through her hair, and she could feel the pounding of his heart, could hear the low groan he made in his throat.

He rocked his lower body against her, and she felt a deep tremor cresting through her pelvis. A soft whimper escaped her. She arched back, and he lifted his mouth from hers and ran his lips across her jaw and down her throat.

Carter could feel the thin threads of his control near the breaking point. It would be so easy to just let go, to let this thing run its course and to hell with the consequences.

But he knew this wasn't the time or the place. There were two impressionable little girls inside the house who could come looking for their parents at any moment.

He gently kissed her lips one last time. Raising his head, he looked down to find her eyes shining up at him. Her mouth was red and lush, lips parted slightly, and he felt hot tendrils of desire mix with some softer emotion that welled up from deep inside him.

The desire was welcome. It was something he could understand and accept.

But the tender emotion? It was crazy! Mild affection and respect were all he wanted to feel for any woman. Yet Jenny did no more than smile at him, and he came alive with feelings.

Small wonder he was having trouble keeping things in perspective.

She turned her face away. "Something's happening here," she whispered, breathless. "Something I didn't count on."

"I know." He let her go and stepped back. "Don't be shy with me, Jenny. Look at me."

She turned her face toward his, and he saw that her cheeks were flushed and her eyes overbright. "I'm not being shy." She laughed softly. "I'm a little embarrassed. This kind of thing just doesn't happen to me. And I'm not sure it's such a good idea."

Carter meant to agree with her, but when he spoke, something entirely different came out. "It's been a long time, hasn't it?"

Her eyes widened. "If you mean getting turned on"—she laughed self-consciously—"then yes. I thought I'd forgotten how to . . . you know."

"You are a refreshingly honest woman, Jenny."

"I try to be."

For a moment he stared at her, gazing into those warm brown eyes that seemed to draw him into their depths. He lowered his gaze. What the hell was he going to do with her? She wasn't meant for casual affairs, and he didn't want anything more.

Some strange, unidentifiable emotion lodged in his throat. It would be best to leave now, he thought, and keep his distance from her. Before it was too late.

Still, he did not move. He could only stare at her. From somewhere inside the house came the laughter of children and the barking of a dog, but that, the whisper of the wind through the trees, and the smell of spring in the air seemed distant. Everything seemed distant and unimportant but her.

Jenny, he thought over the blood pounding in his head, *I've already let you get too close.*

EIGHT

Two evenings later Jenny was in the kitchen preparing dinner. The kids were playing up in Lara's room. Carter was in her pantry, stripped down to his shirtsleeves, whistling a merry little tune.

The good news as far as she was concerned was that he didn't seem annoyed by her animals anymore. Carter tolerated Rags the puppy and Miss Kitty playing chase around his legs, T-Beau's chattering, and Happy's demands for attention.

She'd been surprised and rather touched that he'd brought gifts for the animals that night: rawhide bones for the dogs, a chemical-free grown rose for T-Beau, and catnip for the cats. However, she still didn't know whether to laugh or be insulted by the present he'd eagerly bestowed upon her. It was a self-help book, titled *1001 Ways to Organize Yourself*, and it promised fast, effective relief for common clutter, procrastination, and every organizational ailment.

"You're going to find that it's an indispensable guide," Carter had told her with a perfectly straight face. To demonstrate how simple it was to establish the routines in the book, he'd offered to organize her pantry.

It had seemed harmless enough to her, so she'd murmured, "Whatever floats your boat. Go for it."

Jenny dropped a slice of hard-boiled egg. T-Beau pounced on it and gobbled it up. "Throw me something, mister," he said, looking at her for more.

"That's all you get, silly bird." She blew him a kiss, then went back to putting the spinach salad together and thinking about Carter.

The bad news was that she was beginning to fall for him. She couldn't tell him that, though. For a woman who took pride in her honest nature, her silence on something so important seemed dishonest. But she didn't believe he wanted to hear something like that from her.

Perhaps he would think she loved too easily. It was true that she did. He simply wouldn't understand that she lived on emotion. He might even distance himself from her, because he wasn't comfortable with the verbal expression of feelings.

She had invited him into her life by challenging him to be her coleader of the Sunshine Girls, by becoming the after-school caretaker of his daughter, by encouraging friendship. That was something she couldn't forget. If she truly fell in love with him and he wanted nothing more from her than a few passionate kisses and simple friendship, then it was her problem, not his. So she couldn't tell him how she felt.

It was just unfortunate that this thing happening to her was crazy and about as subtle as a runaway train down a steep mountainside. She'd worry about that tomorrow, though. Tonight it was too nice having him there with her.

"Jenny," he called out.

"What?" She glanced up to see that he'd poked his head out the pantry door.

"I've shelved and alphabetized your canned goods by category."

"Okay." She watched him cross the room with his little notebook in hand.

"You ought to label the shelves to make restocking easy."

"Uh-huh. I'll run out and buy some labels tomorrow."

He grinned, obviously aware she was just humoring him. "I know it sounds compulsive."

"You're right, it does."

"But it will make finding things easier." He leaned against the counter beside her. "Once you establish the system, it will save you time." He lifted his hand and rubbed a strand of her hair between his fingers, and the intimate gesture made her breath catch in her throat.

"If you say so."

"Trust me, it's a good idea. A little organization will make your life easier."

She smiled, looking up at him through her lashes. "Carter, were you the kind of kid who carefully peeled the wrapping paper off your Christmas presents?"

It made him laugh, long and lazily, and he nodded. "Yeah, I did. My mother liked to save the paper and the bows."

She shook her head. "I'm always too excited to find out what's inside the package to be that careful."

"I know." He drew the strand of hair through his fingers again. "You ripped the wrappings off that book in two seconds flat." His smile faded. "I'm sorry you were disappointed by what was inside."

She blushed. "I know you were being thoughtful, and I'm sorry I laughed."

"It's okay."

Jenny stood there looking at him, feeling awkward, then she started to turn away.

His hand flashed out and caught her by the wrist. "If I wanted to give you another gift, what would make you excited enough to rip off the wrapping paper?"

"I adore chocolates. It's the fastest way to my heart."

"I'll remember that." He placed his hand beneath her chin, lifting her face toward his.

She felt the quickening of her heart as he kissed her, teasing her mouth open. His tongue moved against hers, and she shivered, feeling the now-familiar tendrils of desire wind their way through her. She felt drugged and warm as his mouth settled more firmly over hers, hard and demanding. He cupped her head in both hands and kissed her with unapologetic hunger.

A squawk from T-Beau as he swooped over their heads brought her back to reality. She pulled back. "Speaking of good ideas . . ." She felt her heart turn a cartwheel as his fingertips lingered on her cheek. "Speaking of ideas," she forced herself to say casually, "I believe you mentioned that you had a few for the Sunshine Girls."

Carter's gaze held hers for a moment, then he shrugged and turned away, walking across to the fridge and opening it. "I certainly do. The first thing we need to do is give the girls a certain amount of time for each scheduled activity. I'll bring a kitchen timer."

She gave him a blank look. "A kitchen timer?"

He took out a pitcher of iced tea and set it on the counter. "Works great with children. We decide how much time a given activity should take and set the timer. When the bell rings, we go on to the next item on our agenda."

"Are you serious?"

"Trust me. It will work. The water's boiling," he said with a nod at the stove.

She moved by him and dumped pasta into the water. "I'm not sure I like the notion of timing the girls."

"We need to establish a standard structure of order so that the kids know what is expected."

Mutiny, she thought. She fully expected a bloody revolt from the kids.

"I think we should also make an activity dial." He snitched a slice of hard-boiled egg from the salad bowl and ate it.

Hanging from the curtain rod like a miniature vulture, T-Beau squawked and said, "Bugger off, sissy boy."

Carter made a face at the parrot. "Same to you, fella." He glanced at her. "What'd I do to set him off?"

"Hard-boiled eggs are his favorite." Jenny removed Carter's hand from the salad bowl where he'd started to dip in again. "You're stealing the tasty bits he would love to steal for himself. Now, would you please tell me what the heck an activity dial is?"

"It's made out of two cardboard circles, one larger than the other. The large circle records the tasks to be done and the smaller one notes each person's name. Each person is responsible for the task or activity which her name is lined up with."

"Are you serious?" She felt stuck in a groove.

He smiled. "I have one at home for Tiffany as a reminder of what household chores she's supposed to do on what day."

Poor child. Jenny shook her head. "Does she ever get a free day?"

"Sunday. That's our day together. I always plan something special for us like a movie, dinner out, a trip to the zoo."

She smiled. "That's nice."

"By the way, how long will it take to give the fire safety talk on Saturday?" he asked.

"Beats me."

"In that case, I think I should be responsible for giving the talk."

She opened her mouth to protest, then thought better of it. If he wanted the responsibility, he was welcome to it.

He whipped out his little notebook and pen and scribbled something. A reminder to himself, she supposed.

Glancing up at her, he said, "Half an hour ought to be enough time to cover the subject. What about this friendship circle business? How long does that take?"

Her nerves jumped, and she eyed him warily. Efficiency experts could be scary people. And to think she was getting involved with one of them! She must be completely out of her mind.

"It depends." She went back to the stove to check on the pasta and stir the onion, chicken, and garlic mixture simmering in a pan.

"Depends on what?"

She blew out a frustrated breath. "On lots of things. Carter, they talk about their *feelings* and their problems."

He shifted uneasily from one foot to the other. "Oh, right. Feelings."

"You can't set a timer for that," she said, waving a wooden spoon. "Imagine pouring your heart out only to be cut short by a ridiculous bell telling you, 'Sorry, Charlie, but your time is up.'"

He rubbed his jaw. "You may have a point there."

"You're darn right I do. Time anything else you want to, but the friendship circle remains uninterrupted for as long as the girls want to talk. I have to be honest with you, though. I don't think the girls will give two hoots about your activity dial or your kitchen timer."

"Yes, they will. Now, what about snack time?" he asked, seeming undaunted. "How long do you allot for that?"

She shrugged helplessly.

"Okay. How 'bout fifteen minutes?" He jotted that down. "That should give them plenty of time for preparation, consumption, and cleanup."

Jenny threw up her hands, but didn't argue. Let him find out for himself. The kids might be intrigued with his dials and timers, but she doubted that would last. Just when Carter thought it was working, the other shoe would drop. She only hoped he didn't get a concussion when that shoe whacked him on the head.

Carter closed the notebook and tucked it and his pen in his shirt pocket. Regardless of Jenny's lack of enthusiasm, he was satisfied that the next

Sunshine Girls meeting would run smoothly and orderly.

He opened a cupboard and took down four glasses. Setting the table should be a task relegated to the kids, but he liked doing it.

This was only the second dinner invitation he had managed to coax out of Jenny. He fully intended to make such invitations routine. She was a good cook.

In addition, his after-school care arrangement with her was working out so well, he was thinking of making it permanent instead of hiring another full-time housekeeper. Tiffany was blossoming under Jenny's loving and sunny nature. His little girl liked being with Jenny and Lara.

And so did he. He liked Jenny's cozy home and the noise of the kids at play. He liked helping out and setting the table while she bustled around her big kitchen. He was even beginning to like that sassy parrot and the other animals that were constantly underfoot.

The only things Carter did not like were having so few moments alone with her and having to go back to his own silent house. But the weekend was coming, he reminded himself optimistically.

Tiffany and Lara would be staying overnight Saturday with Mrs. Eisen, a neighbor and friend Jenny had introduced him to the day before. Mrs. Eisen was a widow with no grandchildren of her own, and she had immediately accepted Tiffany as another substitute grandchild.

Carter had big plans for Jenny after her sister's dinner party. Big plans.

"Mommy!"

Carter looked up to see Lara and Tiffany standing in the doorway. Something was wrong. It took him a second to put his finger on what it was, then it was all he could do to hold back a startled exclamation. His gaze flew to Jenny. He could see she was just as shocked.

"Well, sugar pie," she said to Lara as she dried her hands on a towel. "You cut your hair." Her tone of voice conveyed no hint of censure, only surprise.

Carter stared openmouthed at her. How could she act so calm? The child's long braids were gone! Her hair looked as though someone had hacked it off with a dull knife.

Lara slowly came forward, her eyes as big as dinner plates. "Me and Tiffany wanted to be twins." She looked on the verge of tears. "I didn't do such a good job, though. My hair doesn't look anything like hers."

The little pixie slowly brought her hand from behind her back. Clutched in her small fist was about six inches of tawny braided hair with the red-and-yellow bands still wrapped around the ends.

Carter inhaled sharply as it finally sank in that the kids had been playing with scissors! Horrified, his gaze flew to his daughter still hovering in the doorway. How many times had he cautioned Tiffany against playing with sharp objects? He opened his mouth to say that, but before he could speak a wail filled the air.

"Mommy, I look awful!" Lara burst into tears.

He closed his mouth as Jenny rushed over to hug Lara.

"No, you don't, sweetie pie," she soothed, going down on her knees to cuddle her daughter. She lifted one hand and fluffed Lara's jagged chin-length locks. "It's just a little bit . . . uneven. We can fix it."

"Really truly?" Lara raised her tear-streaked face.

"Sure, we can. I do wish you had asked me to help you, though."

"Are you mad at me?"

Jenny kissed her daughter's nose. "No, I'm not mad. I *am* disappointed that you didn't ask me to help you, though. My hair-cutting scissors are very sharp, and you know you aren't supposed to touch them."

"Oh, I didn't use your scissors," Lara assured her. "I used the safety scissors that came in my art box that Aunt Mo gave me."

Carter contained an absurd desire to laugh. No wonder the child's hair looked like it had been hacked off.

"Can you fix it right now?" Lara begged. "I want to look just like Tiffany."

"Of course." Jenny got to her feet. "You know,

I think you'll look beautiful with your hair bobbed like hers."

"It isn't easy to cut your own hair," Lara said solemnly as she slipped her hand into her mother's.

Jenny laughed. "No, it isn't." She glanced back and smiled at Carter. "Would you mind keeping an eye on dinner for me?"

"Don't worry, I can handle it."

She guided her daughter toward the door. There she put her free arm around Tiffany's shoulders, and he heard her say, "Would you like to help too, Miss Tiffy?"

Carter watched her and the children until they were out of sight. He was impressed. Jenny had handled the situation without scolding, criticizing, or peppering Lara's self-worth with buckshot.

Somewhere in the house he heard laughter. He found himself feeling warm and content as he listened.

It was then that he knew whatever he felt for Jenny was more intense than he wanted. It was petrifying and exhilarating. It filled him, seeping into him like the warm laughter coming from somewhere in the house.

A woman like her would never just stop loving a man, he thought wistfully. Loving was too ingrained in every fiber of Jenny's being.

His plans for Saturday night underwent a change. A simple seduction of Jenny wasn't going to be enough.

❖————————————————❖

"I feel so sorry for Dad. He seems sad and lost," Sarah, the red-haired moppet, was saying.

This was the moment Carter had been dreading. It was Saturday morning, and he wished he were anywhere in the world rather than sitting on the floor surrounded by little girls talking about their *feelings*.

He'd done all right so far. The meeting had progressed smoothly enough. The girls had been reasonably well-behaved and attentive during the fire safety discussion.

He had lost control over them only three times. First he'd made the mistake of asking who wanted to demonstrate the drop and roll method of putting out a fire on one's clothing. They'd gone wild. Seven of them had dropped to the floor, screaming and yelling, writhing as though in agony. Tiffany had been the only exception. She'd sat hugging her knees and giggling like crazy. Ten minutes had been wasted trying to calm them down again.

A full-scale mutiny had erupted when he had attempted to instruct them on the use of the kitchen timer and the activity dial. They'd practically booed him out of the room. Jenny had saved his bacon by appealing to JoJo's take-charge nature and appointing her activity chairperson in charge of the activity dial.

JoJo had pronounced the kitchen timer the

most moronic idea she'd ever heard. The others had loudly agreed with her.

The third disaster had occurred when Margaret accidentally kicked Bunny. Carter's shin was still sore from the swift kick he'd received when he'd pulled the two apart. It had been another accident —Bunny had been aiming for Margaret.

To his chagrin, Jenny was the one who had managed to restore some sense of order after each disruption. With a skill that was half Mother Teresa and half Rambo, she had somehow maneuvered the group from one activity to another. She'd assigned leaders, set tasks, and found something to praise in each child's performance.

If he hadn't seen it with his own eyes, Carter wouldn't have believed she could do it. He'd found himself admiring her ability to handle such a diverse group of children without breaking into a sweat or screaming bloody murder.

Now, they were talking about *feelings*. He made a concentrated effort not to squirm. He'd rather break up a dozen fights than be in the position he was now.

"What do you think, Carter?" he heard Jenny ask.

He started and gave her a helpless look.

Apparently, she guessed he'd missed too much of the conversation to take a stab at answering her question. "Sarah," she said with a nod at the redheaded child, "feels responsible for her dad's unhappiness. She thinks that going to live with him would make him feel less sad and lonely. Perhaps you could give her a father's point of view."

Carter's heart sank. His gaze flickered over the group. They were looking to him for answers. "Have you talked to your dad about it?" he asked.

Sarah shook her head. "I kinda talked to my mom. One day, when I was in the car with her, I threw a monster temper tantrum. I cried and carried on about wanting to live with Dad. Mom stopped the car and said they had decided that *she* was to have custody of me and that was that."

The poor child, Carter thought. She was confused and terrified, thinking she had the power to make choices that should rightfully be made by adults.

"Your parents are grown-ups and they have had to make some hard decisions," he said gently. "They must think they're doing what's best for you by having you live with your mother." He paused and took a deep breath. "Your father may be feeling sad and lonely right now. But you can't compensate for that. He has to work it out himself. You aren't responsible for how either of your parents feel."

Sarah's face puckered.

Carter's heart sank even lower. She was going to cry! His first friendship circle and he'd already screwed up! He couldn't handle this. Emotions and tears and . . .

"I don't know what compensate means," Sarah said.

She wasn't going to cry!

"It means to make up for," he told her.

"Oh, okay. I get it. I don't have to take care of Dad, 'cause he's an adult and he can take care of himself." Sarah leaned back on her hands, looking as though a burden had been lifted off her small shoulders.

An enormous sense of relief swept through Carter. Maybe he could handle this feeling stuff after all.

He glanced at Jenny. She was smiling at him, beaming her approval. He felt a sizzling heat of awareness as he held her gaze for a long moment. Her eyes became warm pools of desire, and it was like staring at the startling intensity of his own needs. His heartbeat, already thudding hard, became more rapid.

Tonight, he would see her at her sister's dinner party. It would be an adult evening, no kids. In his mind, it was a date, the first of many with this special woman who brought such excitement to his life.

"My mom's got a new boyfriend," Kamika piped up.

Carter's gaze flew to the child. He blanched, fearing he'd be asked to say something on that subject. No, no, no, no. *Don't ask my opinion*, he silently pleaded.

His fears were unfounded. As he sat back, listening and observing the children, he came to an awareness of how important it was for females to feel supported. It made them happy when their feelings were validated.

He felt a body cuddle up to him and glanced down. Cheryl smiled and slipped her chubby hand in his. He smiled back.

This child seemed the neediest of the group. She clung and demanded constant attention, and he couldn't help wondering what her home life was like.

Carter sought out Tiffany. She hadn't said a word since they'd sat down in the friendship circle. Was she afraid to talk about her feelings in front of him? It hadn't occurred to him to tell her that she could say anything she wanted without fear of hurting his feelings.

He'd assumed she knew. Dumb, dumb, dumb. How could she know, if he hadn't told her?

An arrow of pain shot through him. He hadn't grown up in a family that openly discussed feelings, and neither had Carol. Maybe that was why Tiffany had such a difficult time expressing hers. He was certain now that was one of the reasons his marriage had ended.

A classic failure to communicate, he thought in self-disgust. It mortified him to think a clichéd situation had killed his relationship with someone he'd promised to love, honor, and cherish forever.

Laughter broke in to his startling revelations. He looked around and saw that the group was breaking up. They were through? Already? He glanced at his watch. It was time to go.

He got to his feet with some difficulty, since Cheryl didn't seem to want to let him go.

She held on to his leg and stared up at him. "Are you coming back next week?"

He smiled and lightly snatched at the tip of one ragged pigtail. "Of course I'm coming back next week. I'm your new coleader."

Her moon face radiated a smile that showed she'd lost two of her front baby teeth. "I like you." Her chubby arms hugged the daylights out of his leg.

"Cheryl, my little pumpkin," Jenny said, coming to his rescue. "Your grandmother is here."

" 'Kay. Bye, Mr. Dalton. See you next Saturday."

"Bye, Cheryl."

When they were alone except for Lara and Tiffany, Jenny gave him a rueful smile. "Thank you for being so patient with Cheryl. I know her tendency to cling can be wearing, but she needs attention so badly."

He stepped closer and let his fingertips graze her cheek. "I could tell that she does. She's the kind of kid someone needs to take home and love, isn't she?"

He could tell she was surprised by his understanding by the way her eyes widened. Then she smiled. It was more radiant than the one Cheryl had given him. "Yes, she is."

"What's her story?" he asked, glancing at the

thin, stoop-shouldered woman following Cheryl out the door.

"Her mother deserted her. Her father's in jail. She lives with her grandmother. Mrs. Dale is a nice person, but she has serious health problems and taking care of Cheryl seems to be more than she can handle at this stage of her life."

Carter felt a sharp pain in the region of his heart. "There's no one else in the family who could take her in?"

"No one else wants her." She took both his hands in hers and looked up at him. "You did good today. I'm so proud of you. You didn't lose your cool when things got out of hand. You were kind to Cheryl. You really helped Sarah feel better because of what you told her." She paused, and a teasing light crept into her eyes. "You didn't even pout when the kids rejected your kitchen timer."

He laughed. "Thanks."

It was all he could say, even though his heart swelled with emotion, even though he wished he could tell her how much that simple bit of praise meant to him.

Maureen and Mark Robbins lived in the heart of Greensboro's exclusive Irving Park neighborhood, which smelled of old money and Southern gentility. Carter could feel the presence of time and grandeur in their French Normandy-style house. It was in its massive size and the circular tower, in the Italian marble fireplaces and the library with its English oak paneling, even in the quiet ticking of the clocks.

Cocktails were served to twenty guests in the sunroom by the castle's unlikely royalty: a third grade schoolteacher who looked like a leggy blond starlet, and a stockbroker who looked more like he ought to be lecturing private-school boys on the subject of dead poets.

"You didn't tell me your sister lived in a castle," he murmured to Jenny.

She laughed. "It does look like one, doesn't it? Three generations of the Robbins family have lived in this house. As the saying goes, my sister married well. Mark's family has its golden fingers in everything from textiles to investment banking.

"I'll take you on a tour later. This place has six and a half bathrooms. Each one is covered in European tiles of a different color. The half bath is one of the secrets of the house. It's hidden behind the oak paneling in the library. Lara loves to hide in there when she brings her friends over."

"Of all the unusual features of this house, you're impressed with the bathrooms?" he teased.

"When your plumbing is old and cranky, and your toilets literally work on a string and a prayer, you learn to appreciate a great bathroom. Oh, no," she finished with a groan.

"What?"

"Rhonda just spotted us."

"Who?"

"The lady in the pink sequins and diamonds. Her husband is Mark's partner."

"Yoo-hoo! Sugar, it's been ages." Rhonda enveloped Jenny in a glittering hug. From a distance, Carter noticed, she was an attractive, though garishly dressed, woman. At close range, however, her tanned skin had a coarse and grainy look.

The woman turned and looked him up and down with a speculative gleam in her eyes. "And you must be Jenny's new man. Maureen's told us all about you."

Carter blinked in surprise. He glanced at Jenny and saw her flinch.

"I'm Rhonda Sutter. You can call me Rhonda." She threw her arm around Jenny and gave her a squeeze. "Isn't our girl here just the sweetest little ole thing you ever saw? Wouldn't she make some lucky fella a divine wife?"

A hot tide of color swept into Jenny's cheeks. "Rhonda, I heard your daughter has been accepted at Duke. Congratulations. You must be so proud."

Carter recognized her embarrassment. He had an inkling of what was going on. Her sister had enlisted her friends to help her play matchmaker for Jenny. On one hand, he was flattered and amused. On the other, he felt very nervous and cornered.

By the time dessert was served, Jenny wished she'd resisted the impulse to ask Carter to be her

dinner partner. The cocktail hour had been inter-
minable, and dinner was even worse. Her head was
aching like a son of a gun.

"Jenny is a great cook," Maureen gushed to
Carter.

Jenny shot her sister a murderous look. In return she got a beatific smile.

Another woman, who was a mutual friend of
Jenny and Maureen's, chimed in enthusiastically.
"She's a wonderful mother too. I know there's
nothing more she'd love than having a husband of
her own to take care of."

A murmur of agreement went around the table.
Her cheeks burning, Jenny squelched an urge to
throw her napkin over her head and hide.

"She's a singular treasure," Carter responded
smoothly.

She sneaked a peek at him. He was easily the
most handsome man in the room. He looked wonderful in his double-breasted navy suit, light blue
shirt, a red-patterned tie and matching silk hand-
kerchief tucked just so in his breast pocket.

His manners were as flawless as his appearance.
All night long, she had been embarrassed by bla-
tant efforts to pique his interest in her. But he had
endured with gentlemanly grace every gushing
comment, every attempt to shove her down his
throat.

"I just hope," Maureen said, "that someday my
sister will find someone as wonderful as my Mark
to love and cherish." Her gaze settled on her hus-

band seated at the opposite end of the table. They traded a glance that was so filled with unabashed love that Jenny forgot her embarrassment.

A lump rose up in her throat. It was a joy to witness two people showing such love so openly. It was a joy she feared she would never experience. She glanced at Carter, who was also watching the silent exchange between husband and wife.

As though feeling her eyes upon him, he met her gaze, and he smiled. It was a slow, mysterious smile that barely touched his mouth but turned his eyes into cobalt flames. It was a magician's smile, one that conjured seductive secrets she could only imagine; a smile that promised he would share those secrets with her and only her.

His mesmerizing gaze held hers for just a moment, but in that span of time Jenny was aware of him at every level on which a woman could possibly be aware of a man. She felt more alive than she ever had before, and she knew she could not turn away from what was happening to her. If she didn't seize the opportunity to explore the promise of the magic and the secrets in Carter's eyes, she knew she would spend the rest of her life wondering what she had missed.

Jenny made her decision.

Life had thrown Carter Dalton into her path, and she wanted him.

She was coming to love him.

If nothing came of the relationship, if they were too different to make a go of it, then she'd deal with the situation. Her heart had been broken before, and she had survived.

At eleven that night, Jenny stood on her front porch feeling too keyed up to go inside just yet. Carter had left her sister's house first, claiming he had work to do at home for a new client. She had the depressing notion that had been just an excuse to get away from the dinner party from hell.

The sound of an expensive engine caught her attention, and she turned to see a black Porsche pull into her driveway. She sucked in her breath as the unfamiliar automobile parked behind her minivan.

The car door opened. Her brain registered the threat of attack and sent her body a fight-or-flight message. She backpedaled toward the front entry, her hand tightening on the palm-size canister of Mace attached to her key chain.

She thumbed the safety button on the canister.

"Get back in your car and get out of here!" she yelled. "I've got Mace."

NINE

"Good. I'm glad to know you aren't defenseless." Carter's voice was dark and gritty in the shadows. "A woman alone can't be too careful."

Jenny stood glowering furiously as he came toward her. Her heart still raced, and her nerves were stretched tight. "Good heavens, you nearly scared me to death."

"I didn't mean to scare you."

"Well, you did. I didn't recognize the Porsche. I thought you drove a Buick."

"I do most of the time. The Porsche isn't a family car." He stood at the bottom of the steps, staring up at her. "I'm sorry I left the party early."

"You didn't miss a thing, believe me."

One side of his mouth lifted in a quirky grin. "Who was that woman with the awful horse laugh?"

Jenny chuckled and rolled her eyes. "The wife

of the gentleman who kept blowing cigar smoke in your face. Investment clients of Mark's. Don't you have work waiting for you at home?"

His grin became rueful. "I lied."

"I know."

"I really am sorry. It wasn't nice of me to go running out like that."

"No, but it was smart. If it hadn't been my sister's party, I'd have bailed out after cocktails."

He walked up the steps. "Will you quit making it easy for me, and just let me apologize?"

She laughed. "Okay."

He stood in front of her. "I was a rat and I'm sorry."

"I accept."

Her eyes locked on his, Jenny felt every inch of her skin become acutely sensitized, yearning for his touch. "I owe you an apology for Maureen and her guests. I never dreamed she would get her friends involved in . . ."

"Singing your praises?" he said helpfully.

She nodded. "Mo has never done that before. I was embarrassed. You must have felt like a fox trapped by a pack of baying hounds. I'm really sorry."

"You have nothing to apologize for. It wasn't your fault."

"You were uncomfortable. I *am* sorry about that."

He looked at her for a long moment, his eyes hungry, the expression on his face a mixture of longing and uncertainty. "I admit I left because it was getting to me. It wasn't because I didn't want to be with you."

"What are you doing here, Carter?"

"I wanted"—his voice went lower and huskier —"to see you. I couldn't stay away." He edged closer, and she felt sexual tension snapping like a live wire. "It's been driving me crazy all night. I have to know."

"Know what?" Her body arched toward him of its own accord, but didn't touch.

"Do you have anything on under that jacket?" He lifted one hand to her chin and tilted her face up so that she was forced to continue gazing into his hypnotic blue eyes.

Jenny swallowed hard. "A black lace bra. You know, you've seen it." She wanted him to kiss her, to put his beautiful mouth on hers.

"Did you ever find the matching panties?" He grasped her upper arms, then slid his hands downward in a caress, stopping at her fingers.

"I'm wearing those too." Jenny felt herself flushing. Her gaze slid away from the flare of heat in his eyes.

His hands tightening on hers, Carter was all too aware of the sensual hunger gnawing at him. She looked stylish and sexy in a long silky black jacket worn over about four inches of mauve silk skirt, hose that matched the skirt, and black spiky heels. His gaze slid lower, to the fair skin revealed by the V neck of her jacket. To look at her was an experience in pure sensualism. He felt his instant response in the tightening of his body.

"I've never wanted anything the way I want you." He touched her lips with his, but didn't actually kiss her. She sighed his name against his mouth. He drew in her warm breath, running the tip of his tongue across her bottom lip. The air seemed charged with sexual energy that was raw and nerve-racking.

He wanted to taste the sweet fragrance of her fair skin, to fill his palms with her small, firm breasts. He wanted to savor every part of her, inside and out. He wanted her laughter and her passion.

"Invite me in." He lowered his head and took her mouth with bruising urgency. A little bit of heaven. That's what it would be like to be inside her. She didn't resist the fury of his kiss or the eagerness of his hands sliding up and over her back.

"Yes, yes," she whispered against his lips. She arched into him, gripping his shoulders, then her arms curved around his neck.

Jenny, Jenny . . . Her name sang through his mind as her sweet tongue danced against his. He was dizzy with the taste of her, with wanting her so much, he could barely breathe. She was just as eager as he, clinging to him as the flames of passion burned brighter and hotter.

She pressed against him, her fingers sliding into his hair. He brought one hand up her back to the nape of her neck, his fingers caressing the delicate skin as he locked her in a deeper, more intense kiss. His other hand drifted up her torso to cup her breast. It was firm and full, the nipple aroused to a hard peak. She moaned deep in her throat, and the sound drove him half crazy with desire.

"Give me your keys," he whispered against her lips.

"Okay."

He released her to unlock and open the door. Once inside the foyer, he noticed the house was oddly silent. No dog jumped on him. No parrot dive-bombed his head. "Where are the animals?"

She smiled. "Happy and Rags are bedded down in the kitchen. T-Beau is in his cage."

"So it's just you and me."

"Just you and me."

He lifted her hand and touched his lips to the vulnerable inside of her wrist. "You want me tonight, don't you?"

"Yes."

"But do you want to get involved with me? Not just for tonight but for as long as it lasts?"

"No," she said honestly. "But I'm going to anyway."

"Why, Jenny?" He drew her loose hair back and kissed the side of her throat lingeringly. "Why are you going to anyway? You strike me as the kind of woman a man ought to marry and cherish."

Jenny's heart twisted, and she had to close her eyes for a moment. "Because I—" Her voice cracked and she swallowed. *Because I already care too much. Because I think I've fallen in love with you.* "Because you make me feel reckless. Because I want to."

"We have nothing in common." His eyes glittered behind half-lowered lids. He ran his hands slowly up and down her arms. She shivered.

"That's true," she whispered. She'd told herself that dozens of times, but her heart didn't care. Neither did her body. It was as tight as a bowstring, her breasts swollen, the tips stiff and aching, crying out for his touch.

"Except that we're crazy for each other," he murmured.

She raised her hand to his face, resting her palm on his cheek. "We're friends. We're attracted to each other. I don't always know what I'm doing, Carter. But I know I want you . . . for as long as it lasts."

"You might regret it. I—"

She stopped his words by pressing her fingers to his mouth. "We'll keep it simple. Friends. Lovers. No matter what happens, no regrets."

He kissed her fingers. "You're unique. I knew it the first time we met. I wanted you then."

"I was a sweaty mess."

"A sexy, sweaty mess." He laughed softly as he scooped her up into his arms.

Surprised, she clutched at his shoulders. "Put me down. You'll drop me."

"Never. Where to?"

"Upstairs. Second door on the right."

He carried her as though she were weightless. With only the dim glow of the foyer lamp to light the way, the intimacy of the moment intensified. She was acutely aware of being cradled in Carter's arms, held snugly against his warm body.

She clung to him and buried her face in the hollow between his throat and shoulder. Shutting her eyes, she let the shadows spin around her. The fine woven fabric of his suit coat teased her cheek, and she breathed in the fresh, spicy scent of his cologne.

Something that felt so right couldn't be wrong, she told herself. All thoughts of future farewells drifted from her mind. Tomorrow would take care of itself. It always did. She could only throw herself into this new adventure with an energy and a joy that wasn't tainted by regrets. And she would simply hope for the best.

A tremor went through her as her feet once again touched the floor. She opened her eyes and found that they were in her bedroom. The drapes were drawn and the lamp on the nightstand was on. "Sorry about the mess," she murmured, seeing the room through his eyes: the unmade bed and the clothes she'd rejected earlier piled on a chair. "I couldn't decide what to wear."

"It's perfectly . . . you, Jenny." He held her hands and stepped back, as if the touching of their aroused bodies was too much for his control.

"Are you saying I'm a perfect mess?" she teased.

He smiled. "You're perfectly beautiful."

She shook her head. "You don't have to say that. I know I'm plain. I'm too skinny. My breasts are too small. My freckles are ugly."

"You are beautiful to me," he answered softly, his eyes locking with hers. "I love the way your body is made. You're sleek and lean. You've got such a tiny waist." He put his hands there and stroked her. "You're sweet and tempting and sexy." He smiled. "Even your freckles turn me on. I've had a few fantasies about kissing every freckle on your body." He leaned down and began kissing a path across her nose.

"Oh, Carter." She believed him. He really did think she was beautiful. Her heart was in her throat as she smiled.

He slipped his hands up her arms and drew her toward him. "Nervous?"

"Terrified! Three years is a long time."

"Three years," he murmured.

Some small part of his mind kept telling Carter he was asking for serious trouble, getting involved with Jenny. She made him remember what it was like to care deeply for a woman. To love emotionally as well as physically was something he didn't want to think about right now.

He gazed down into her big brown eyes. "I want you wrapped around me, naked and soft and warm. I want you moving with me, melting around me."

Her eyes widened and he smiled, then pulled her against him. "I want to make it good for you. I want to make you happy."

"You do make me happy." She leaned into him, and her sigh of pleasure strained his willpower.

He lowered his mouth to hers and kissed her, slowly and lazily, savoring the sweetness of her. His body was so aroused, it hurt to breathe.

"I'm so ready for you, I'm half out of my mind with it," he said in a gritty whisper. He felt her breath catch and raised his head. Her eyes were heavy-lidded with passion. "This first time is going to be deep and hard and fast. We're going to set each other on fire."

Jenny could already feel the magic and the fire he promised. She felt weak and dizzy and shaken right down to the core of her being.

"But the second time . . . the second time will be the long, slow kind that only gets better. We're going places we've only dreamed about, Jenny."

He started unbuttoning her silk jacket, his gaze holding hers. When he'd slipped the last button free, he slid the jacket from her shoulders. He kissed her, drawing moist swirls with his tongue that made her ache for more. She helped him ease the jacket down her arms until the garment dropped to the floor.

"I've had some erotic dreams about you wearing nothing but this bra and a smile," he murmured, nudging off one strap, then the other. "Reality is better." He undid the catch in the front and parted the lacy cups with the tips of his fingers.

Swallowing hard, she shrugged and let the bra fall, baring herself to the waist. She saw Carter's eyes narrow with passion as he gazed at her.

His hands were large and gentle, his skin a darker hue than her pale flesh. She watched his hands slowly move to the waistband of her skirt. He found the side zipper and drew it down. She placed her hands on top of his, and together they inched the skirt past her hips. She kicked off her heels and stepped out of the skirt.

His hands cupped her breasts, and she had to fight to catch her breath. His touch heated her body to a blistering degree. Her nipples were full and hard, aroused by the brush of his thumbs. She could barely stand upright as sensations spiked within her, darting throughout her, tugging at the deepest, most intimate places. She had wanted this, his hands on her, his kiss . . .

Carter struggled against the raw emotion crowding his chest, filling him with a fever he knew only she would cure. Forcing down the rising pressure of need that had been punishing his body, he captured her face between his hands, touching her with every bit of grave reverence he felt. He caressed her cheekbones, traced the sprinkling of light freckles across her nose, ran his fingers over the sensual curve of her mouth.

When he stroked over her throat to her shoulders, he heard her soft moan. Her small hands gripped his arms as she fought a shudder that shook her slender body. The power she held over him touched him deeply. Gazing down into her passion-filled eyes, he felt a sharp tug in his loins that were already heavy and full.

His breath left him with an explosive groan, and he kissed her hungrily. He lifted her against him, rotating his pelvis.

"Hurry," she whispered. Slipping her arms around his neck, she returned his kiss eagerly, cupping him between her thighs and pressing her silken length against him. "Please don't make me wait."

He was only half aware of stripping panty hose and black lace panties down her smooth, shapely legs. He took one stride forward, then eased her onto the cool pastel sheet covering the bed. She moaned again, her voice catching on his name, as she tried to pull him down with her.

"In a moment, love," he said, catching her wrists. He bent down to kiss her lightly. "Just let me look at you." How could he ever have thought she was too small, too plain? She was beautiful. Smooth and sleek. So full of energy and life. Her skin was so warm, so warm and soft in his hands.

"I've wanted you since the first time I saw you," he told her as he began undressing. "It's a hunger that's been clawing at me day and night."

A smile trembled on her lips. He'd wanted to see her eyes like this, intensely focused on only him, alight with the passion that caught fire and raged between them. Her gaze never left him as he unbuttoned his shirt and removed his tie.

"Hurry, Carter," she whispered.

"I've wanted to know what you look like. What you feel like." The desire that swirled around him seemed as complex and dangerous. It was fierce and heartless. He wanted to take her quickly, instantly. But he forced himself to slow down.

Jenny watched him with an open heart that was ready to take him in. He was beautiful. She loved the long, hard lines of his body.

She had no defenses left. Tonight was special. She would give him everything, including her secret love. She thought of nothing but him, not the past, not the future. And perhaps, he would give more of himself than he intended.

"Were you so certain this would happen?" she asked as he took a foil packet of protection from his pocket.

His mouth softened into a smile. "Not certain. Just hopeful."

It was the right thing to say. She smiled and held out her arms.

Carter lay down beside her. With a tenderness

that surprised him, he gathered her into his arms. He skimmed his lips over her bare shoulders, drinking in the texture, as smooth as silk, and her scent that was just as tantalizing. She suddenly seemed so small and fragile. After a moment's hesitation, he brought his mouth to merge with hers.

The stroke of her hands over his body made him burn. He covered her mouth again, hotly, urgently, catching her full lower lip with his. Sensations ruled him. His body contracted with a wild surge of pleasure.

"Oh, Carter, I want you so badly," she cried out, straining against him. "It's been so long . . ."

She cried out again as he cupped one of her breasts in his hand. He teased the nipple with his thumb, and she arched her back. She moaned when spirals of heated sensation darted outward and downward, traveling to the core of her femininity. Instinctively, she raised her leg, rubbing it intimately against his.

"You feel so good," he murmured, then lowered his head to kiss each breast.

Moaning, she gave herself over to the hedonistic upheaval going on in her body. She'd never known a man could give so freely with his hands and his mouth, as if he wanted nothing more than to please her and drive her out of her mind with his promise of passion.

Wherever his desire took him, she was waiting and willing. Carter had never experienced anything, anyone like Jenny. She sizzled with heat and arousal. He could feel her throbbing pulse wherever he touched, whenever he tasted her skin. She was so open to his loving, so free and wildly uninhibited. Her touch was honest, generous, and as natural as breathing.

"I don't think I'll ever get enough of you," she whispered, arching under him like a bow. She pushed herself against him as he continued to suckle her. He slipped his hand between her thighs, and she opened for him. He found her pleasure point. She bucked upward, groaning, as he massaged her, all the while his mouth tugged greedily on her breast.

"Let it happen, sweetheart," he whispered, moving his mouth to the valley between her breasts. "Don't think. Don't hold back."

He felt the pressure building in her body with each shiver. He heard it in each shuddering breath she took. Quickening his caress, he brought her to the pinnacle of intensifying pleasure. She called out his name, her voice a ragged cry of release. He held her trembling body, kissing her eyes, her nose, her open mouth.

She touched his face and gazed into his eyes. "I've never felt anything so . . . wonderful."

"You like my touch?"

"I love it."

For a heart-stopping moment, Carter thought he was going to lose it. Along with his passion that she accepted so freely, he gave her a piece of his soul.

She smiled in a way that made him pray for the willpower to hang on a little longer. "I hope you like my touch," she said. She slipped her hand caressingly down his body and circled his manhood with her fingers. He throbbed beneath her silken touch as she moved her hand over him.

The tight control he kept over his will and emotions vanished. Carter crushed his mouth to hers with rough desperation. His hands raced over her until she was writhing beneath him. She lifted her knees to grip him by the hips. Then he thrust himself forward, and gave a low groan as he sank fully and deeply into her.

He whispered coaxing words to her as he made love to her with a driving passion, as deep and hard and fast as he had promised. Each thrust of his hips brought him deeper into her silken warmth and nearer to heaven.

He raised his head, wanting to see what the feel of him did to her. Her face was flushed with pleasure. Her eyes were open and fixed on his. A tremor went through her body. A second tremor was stronger, and tore a cry from her. It was incredibly erotic, holding her tightly and watching her cataclysmic completion. It drove him over the edge, and his own release came in floods of unspeakable pleasure.

Carter didn't know how long they dozed, wrapped in each other's arms. The room was warm and still. Soon the dark would give way to light.

A wave of protectiveness passed over him when he looked at Jenny's sleeping face. It broke his heart just a little.

He smiled to himself, but he feared they would both be hurt by their carnal feelings. What a cruel joke on them both, he thought, that they should find each other so tempting.

He had learned the hard way that passion and love didn't last. The lesson had been confusing and painful, and he didn't want to know that kind of pain again. Nor did he want to inflict such pain on Jenny.

She deserved better.

She stirred in her sleep, and he felt the warm pressure of her body seeking him. Her arm slipped across his chest.

It felt so good to lie beside her, to tuck her head against his neck. He kissed the top of her head, loving the soft silkiness of her hair against his lips.

"There's a reason you came into my life," she murmured sleepily.

He smiled. "And what would that be?"

"To make me feel beautiful and more alive as a woman than I've ever felt before."

Breath caught in his throat. Words spoken in passion sometimes held little meaning, but he could read the truth in her honest pixie face. She really meant what she said.

He wanted to tell her how good she made him feel. He wanted to tell her how much he cared for her. But the words stuck in his throat. He tightened up inside. Baring his soul would leave him too open, too vulnerable. Instead of speaking, he kissed her tenderly, hoping she would know a little of what he was feeling through his touch.

She lay back, looking at him with caressing eyes. Her breasts were as fair as the rest of her, the hard nipples flushed a deep rose with arousal. He sat up and leaned over her to kiss the silky brown hair between her legs. Parting her legs with his hands, he kissed the warm flesh open to him.

As she sighed he moved up beside her. He tilted her face to his and kissed her slowly. Her hands swept over him, seeking the heat of his body. She touched his chest, seeming to love its hardness.

Passion grew hot and strong. He slipped his hand downward and found her moist and ready. His body caught fire as her mouth moved against his, growing more insistent.

He forced himself to stop long enough to reach for the protection he'd placed on the table beside her bed. Her eyes remained fixed on him until he again kissed her.

They came together slowly. The rhythm soon quickened, and he claimed her mouth again and again. How could something be so perfect and so precious? he wondered as he drank a moan of pleasure from her lips.

When it was over, she looked up at him. Her eyes glowed. Her smile was filled with sweetness and spent passion. It beckoned a need to love and cherish.

And his heart broke just a little.

TEN

"I *know* I put it here," Jenny muttered, riffling through the stacks of papers, bills, and correspondence on her desk.

So far, she'd found all kinds of things she wasn't looking for: a program from the production of *A Christmas Carol* that she and Lara had attended at UNCG two years ago, a letter she'd written to a high school friend that she'd meant to mail last month, ninety-eight cents, a flashlight with dead batteries, and a pair of pink lace panties. How her underwear had gotten mixed in with her past tax returns was one of life's strange little mysteries.

What she still couldn't find was the folder containing the information she needed to update the membership directory for the church where she was employed. She was certain she'd brought the folder home with her the day before, because she'd intended to start working on the new directory last night. But somehow, she'd never gotten around to it. Now the cotton-pickin' thing was missing in action.

She absently stuffed the panties in her jeans pocket and looked at the disaster area she'd made of her desk. Though she'd rather suck rotten lemons than admit it to Carter, she conceded that he *might* be a teensy-weensy bit right about her lack of organizational skills.

She had spent a frustrating hour hunting for the folder that she should have been able to put her hands on immediately. That was an hour she could have spent working on the project.

Getting organized might not be so bad, she thought, reaching for the self-help book Carter had given her. She'd treated the gift as a joke and had tossed it on the desk and had forgotten about it. She picked it up and read the first sentence.

Are you a procrastinator?

Was she ever.

Do you often wait until the last minute to start a project?

The new church directory was due on Friday. It was Wednesday evening. Oh, yeah, Last Minute might as well be her middle name.

Do you feel overwhelmed by too many details?

This book must have been written for her.

Jenny thumbed back to the index. There was a whole section on getting control of paperwork, calendars, desk organization, filing systems, etc.

Two hours later, the contents of her desk were organized, and she had made a list of supplies she needed for creating a workable filing system. She was pleased with her efforts. She knew where everything was, and she could immediately put her hand on important papers and phone numbers. Being organized would make her life a little easier.

Just like Carter had said it would.

She thought of the way he'd organized her kitchen pantry. He was right about her wasting less time trying to find what she needed. She'd set limits, though, refusing to go overboard by labeling the shelves. He hadn't belittled her for not taking his advice. Instead, he'd respected the limit she'd set.

She was finally beginning to understand the difference between Carter's and Greg's attitudes toward structure, objectives, and organization. One had used them as a means to control her. The other simply advocated them as a means for getting control of one's *own* life.

Jenny smiled as her thoughts turned to Carter. Caring about people came easily to her. Caring about family was as automatic as the beating of her heart. Caring for friends evolved instantly or grew slowly and steadily. She could care about an animal nobody else wanted, or a child for no other reason than the child needed someone to care.

But caring about Carter was different. Every time she was with him, she sensed emotional roots sinking deeper into her heart's fertile soil.

A sigh escaped her. She got up and went to continue the search for the missing folder.

She couldn't believe she was doing this! Jenny thought as she clutched her canvas handbag. She had chosen to stuff a few cosmetics, a toothbrush, a fresh set of underwear, and a nightgown into the largest purse she owned rather than announce her intentions to the world by arriving at Carter's house with an overnight bag.

It had been a week since she'd made love with him. It had been so good. Better than good. Even allowing for the fact that she had been without a man for a very long time, it had been an incredible experience. Unlike anything she had ever known.

It was supposed to be simple being friends and lovers, but it wasn't for her. She was falling in love. Even if she had known last Saturday night that her heart would insist on getting involved, she would still have made love with him.

It amazed her that things could change so fast. One minute she had been completely contented with her life. The next, Carter had entered her world, changing her life by simply being a part of it. Now, she couldn't imagine going through the day without seeing him. Her hopes and dreams were constantly expanding to include him.

Hope. She'd never realized that hope contained an element of fear. Fear that she couldn't have what she wanted most. Fear that he would never see her as more than a friend, more than a lover.

She took a deep breath to steady herself. Then she quickly pressed the doorbell before she gave in to a bad case of jitters and ran for home like a scared little rabbit.

Carter opened the door. He had obviously just finished showering and dressing. His hair was still damp. He was dressed for comfort in black slacks and a cool blue shirt that intensified the cobalt color of his eyes.

She managed a shaky smile. "Hello. You look nice." *Nice* was a picnic in May, according to her sister. Carter looked better than nice. He was the flesh and bones, heart and soul that her dreams were made of.

There was nothing shaky about the smile he gave in return. "You look like the Fourth of July."

"Do you like my dress?" She held out her arms and struck a pose. Tiny white stars were printed on the clingy red cotton knit. She wore the dress cinched at the waist with a woven leather belt. "Lara said it was funky. I'm not sure if that means good or bad." She laughed, and it sounded a bit forced and nervous to her.

"I vote for good." His eyes gleamed as his gaze drifted over her.

Jenny suddenly felt warm. No doubt about it, the look in Carter's eyes was primitive, possessive.

"Are the girls settled in at the Y?" he asked as he took her hand and brought her inside.

"They were playing volleyball when I left." The YMCA had invited the gymnastics class and several church youth groups to participate in an overnight lock-in of fun and games.

He frowned. "Volleyball can get rough. Are you sure there's enough adults supervising them?"

"Yes, I'm sure, Mister Worrywart."

"Loosen up, right?"

She smiled. "Right. No more worrying about the kids. Okay?"

"What kids?" He grinned and gathered her into his arms. "Come here, star-spangled pixie. I haven't even kissed you hello yet."

Jenny felt her senses leaping to life. "No wonder I was feeling neglected."

"We can't have that." He kissed her nose, then raised his head. She loved the way he was regarding her now, his eyes warm with affection, a teasing half smile on his sensual lips. "Is that better?"

"It wasn't quite what I had in mind," she said, tracing his lower lip with her forefinger.

"Maybe you should show me what you had in mind."

"All right." She caught his face between her palms and brought her mouth up to his parted lips. She kissed him deeply, her tongue making sweeping, swirling motions inside his mouth. Her fingers drifted into the damp strands of his black hair.

Something clutched her heart as she kissed him with all the urgency she felt. It was terrifying to want so desperately to tell him she loved him. Suppressing her emotions had been difficult for her ever since she'd woken up from the emotional void she'd experienced during her marriage. With Carter, though, she felt she needed to hold on as tight as she could. He wasn't comfortable with emotions.

After a moment, he raised his head and smiled down at her. "Better?"

"Much better." She swallowed hard and hoped her love didn't show in her eyes. The nervous jitters took hold of her again, and she spoke the first inane thing that came to mind. "You have a lovely home."

"Thank you. Want a tour?"

The interior of his home matched the sleek elegance of its contemporary exterior. Pale walls were set off by impressionist paintings, a color scheme soothing to the eye, and big windows that let in a beautiful view of green lawn and blue sky.

Everything was lovely and tasteful, but just a shade too perfect for her comfort. The chaos of everyday living didn't intrude upon the well-ordered haven of his home. Jenny had an overwhelming urge to do something to leave her mark upon the rooms they walked through, to mess something up—kick her shoes off in the middle of the floor, leave a handprint on one of the pristine, monogrammed white towels in his bathroom, scatter a few magazines, drag some toys off the shelves in Tiffany's pink-and-white storybook bedroom.

The combination kitchen, breakfast nook, and

den came as a pleasant surprise after the elegant but sterile look of the other rooms. White cabinets, a fresh blue-and-white-tile scheme, and fabrics in country French prints made the area a bright and cheerful place in which to work and play.

There she found a few signs that a family really lived in this house. The day's newspaper, a blue coffee mug, and a Barbie doll littered the kidney-shaped work island in the kitchen. A pair of men's athletic shoes and Tiffany's schoolbag lay on a small table near the French doors that led out onto a deck. Books and several toys were scattered about in the den.

"Sorry about the mess," Carter said as he tidied up the newspaper. He stuck the doll under his arm and carried the mug over to the sink.

"If you think this is a mess, I'm surprised you haven't run screaming from my house."

He grinned at her over his shoulder as he rinsed out the mug. "The first time I saw your living room, I thought it had been tossed by burglars."

"Ouch!" She made a face and reached one arm around to grope her back.

"What are you doing?"

"Feeling for the knife."

"Sometimes the truth hurts," he said solemnly, though his eyes twinkled with amusement.

"Unlike some *neat freaks* I know," she said loftily, "I've got better things to do than mop floors all day and chase cobwebs."

"Ah, does that knife in your back still hurt?" He laughed as he walked toward her, the doll still stuck under his arm. "Let me kiss it and make it better."

"Not on your Nelly." She backed away.

He wiggled his eyes like a silent-movie villain. "It wasn't *my* Nelly I was thinking of kissing."

Laughing, she scooted backward through the breakfast nook.

"What is a Nelly anyway?" he asked, following her into the den.

"If you don't know what it is," she teased, "how can you kiss it?"

"Beats me." He paused and gave her a wicked grin. "Hold still, and I'll kiss different spots until we find out where your Nelly is located."

She laughed. "You'll have to catch me first."

"Did I tell you I ran track in high school?" He tossed the doll onto a nearby chair and started toward her with a determined gleam in his eyes.

She turned to run, then stopped dead. "Wow!"

"What?"

"You've got photographs."

He came up beside her and gave her an odd look. "Of course I do. Doesn't everybody?"

"Well, yeah. But this is amazing." She moved closer to examine the display of framed photographs covering the wall behind the sofa. Here was the first real warm and personal touch she'd seen in his house.

Fascinated, she let her gaze drift over whimsical artwork and frames of different textures, shapes, and dimensions. It delighted her to see that there was nothing regimented or organized in the eclectic display. There were turn-of-the-century photographs of people and places mixed in with baby pictures and vacation snapshots. One frame held what she guessed was a first-day-of-school photo of Tiffany attached to the upper right corner of her first paper with cursive writing.

"What are you grinning about?" Carter asked, looping one arm over her shoulders.

"I'm surprised that there's no sense of order, chronological or otherwise, in the way you arranged this display. Why is it that this is the only unstructured thing in your house?"

"I don't know. It just felt right to do it that way. This is what my mother calls a cherished-memories wall." He shrugged and looked sheepish as though he felt slightly embarrassed.

"I love it."

Jenny had known there was deep passion within this structure-oriented man. She had seen it in his eyes and felt it in his touch whenever he kissed her and when he made love to her. Though Carter kept it hidden, she knew he was capable of deep emotions. Now, she also knew he had an even deeper sentimental streak.

"Is that you and your mother?" she asked,

pointing to a picture in a gilded frame. It showed a woman and child at the beach. The woman's face was hidden behind a big strawhat. She was bent halfway over as though she were about to lend a helping hand to the round-bellied toddler at her side.

"Uh-huh. I think I was about two. My bathing trunks were about to fall down. Mom was fussing at Dad to hold his horses until she could pull them up for me." He grinned. "Dad snapped that picture just seconds before the damn things fell down around my ankles."

"You look like you were such a sweet little boy."

"According to my mom, I was hell on two legs."

She smiled and turned to study a portrait of a dark-haired fairy princess of a young woman cradling an infant in her arms. "She's beautiful. Is that Tiffany and her mother?"

Carter moved behind her and encircled her waist with his arms. "Yes."

Jenny turned and hugged him.

He glanced down at her. "What was that for?"

"For being so sensitive." *And because she loved him.*

"Sensitive?" He stared at her. The shadows in his eyes shifted rapidly, as if he were running through a variety of responses in his mind. Abruptly he let go of her and turned from the wall, shaking his head. "You must be mistaking me for some other guy."

"Don't bother denying it, champ. I've got your number now. I've met too many divorced men and women who don't have the sensitivity to openly display photographs of their ex-spouses for their children."

"Look, I want you to know I'm not carrying a torch for Carol. No matter what happened between us, Carol was the mother of my child. The only reason her portrait is there is because I don't want our daughter to forget her mother loved her very much." He turned around again and looked at her searchingly. "It doesn't make you uncomfortable?"

"Not at all." In fact, she had to bite her tongue to keep from blurting out that it made her love him even more. When she had the impulse under control, she said softly, "I think it's a beautiful way to help Tiffany remember her mother."

He moved back to her and brought one hand up to the nape of her neck. "You are one special lady, Jenny Johnson." His mouth brushed hers.

The kiss was subtle, not a storming of her senses, but a careful foray that left her wanting more. She burrowed into the captivating heat of his body. When both his hands closed around her, she caught her breath. It was only then that he slowly filled her mouth, tasting her intimately, possessively. This kiss was a sample, she knew, a claiming and a promise, a forerunner of what they would share that night.

Carter broke free of Jenny's mouth. He felt stunned by the feelings and emotions that filled his heart and mind and body. He'd honestly thought that kind of depth of desire and longing for love was in the past, but he'd been wrong.

"Damn," he muttered. Whatever he was feeling couldn't be love. He wasn't ready to love again.

"Carter, is something wrong?"

"No." There was no way he could explain what was wrong. He didn't understand himself. Better to deny it altogether. Be sensible. Focus on the safety of being friends and lovers.

He forced a smile. "Come see my jukebox."

For a moment she looked as though she wanted to question him further, then she said, "All right."

He led her over to the other side of the room. "I found this baby at an auction. Isn't it a beauty?"

She nodded. "I've haunted a few flea markets in search of treasures among the trash, but I've never been to an auction."

"Someday I'll take you to one."

"I'd like that." She smiled, and the warm sensuality of that smile twisted his stomach into knots. "Does this thing work?" she asked, peering through the glass at the stacks of records inside the jukebox.

"You bet. It's stocked with recordings by Nat King Cole, Ella Fitzgerald, B.B. King, Duke Ellington, and some of the great fifties recording artists like Buddy Holly and the Crickets." He pressed one of the selection buttons. The machine whirled to life, its mechanical arm selected an old 45 record and plopped it down on the turntable.

When Nat King Cole began to sing "Unforgettable," her eyes widened and she sighed. "I love that song."

"Would you like to dance?"

She didn't answer. She just turned and walked into his arms. He held her with an easy familiarity, as though they'd danced together a thousand times before. He felt sixteen again, young and eager and excited by the scent and the feel of a soft female body pressed against him.

Carter tried to keep a tight grip on his emotions. But as they swayed in time to the music, he found it impossible to remain uninvolved. The perfumed warmth of her slender body made him ache all over with wanting.

The song ended, and he slowly released her. When he saw the dreamy expression on her face, he knew the meaning of "starry-eyed."

"You never cease to amaze me." She reached up to graze his cheek with her fingers. Her eyes locked on his mouth, and she moved her fingers there, touching his lips with whisper softness. "Every time I think I've got you figured out, you throw me a curve. Never would I have suspected you were a closet romantic."

Carter felt as though his heart skipped a beat. No one had ever thought of him as sensitive and romantic the way she did. He didn't know how to react. Denial sprang to his lips, and words that tasted as thick as molasses flowed from his mouth. "I'm no romantic, Jenny. I think you're trying to read more into my taste in music than there really is."

"I don't think so." Her dreamy expression changed to one that held a breath-catching moment of naked longing.

He knew that look. *Kiss me.* He knew she wanted him to. The air seemed to vibrate with her unspoken need. He watched her lips part in anticipation as she leaned forward and slid her hand behind his neck, pulling his mouth down to hers.

He surrendered with a groan. The instant their lips touched, he wrapped his arms around her. Then he was lost in the thrusting rhythm of a deep kiss.

Just when Jenny felt as if she were melting inside with love, he pulled back. Opening her eyes, she took in his worried face. "Carter?"

He sighed. It had a defeated sound. "I think I'd better start dinner." His shoulders went ramrod straight as he strode across the room.

Hurt and confused, she stared after him. One minute he'd been with her all the way, as passionately eager as she. The next, he'd shut down and shut her out. What had happened? Had she been too bold? Too needy? Too . . . something? She didn't have a clue.

Pride made her square her own shoulders and

lift her chin a notch higher than usual. She walked into the kitchen and sat down on one of the stools at the blue-and-white-tiled work island. "Is there anything I can do to help?"

"Not a thing," he said without looking at her. "Would you like a drink?"

"Yes, please."

"Coming right up." He took two long-stemmed glasses from a cupboard and got a bottle of white wine out of the refrigerator.

Jenny wasn't much of a drinker, and wine usually made her sleepy. But she readily accepted the crystal goblet he handed her, hoping it would help soothe her jangled nerves.

For a while she sipped her wine and watched him work. Soon he had ingredients neatly lined up beside the appropriate bowls, pans, plates, and utensils. A pile of freshly washed bib lettuce filled a colander in the sink. The makings for a honey-mustard dressing were set out nearby. A loaf of crusty sourdough bread waited on a cutting board. Judging by the number of chicken breasts piled on a platter beside the grill imbedded in the stove top, Carter must have thought he was feeding ten instead of two.

Growing more nervous with the silence, she cleared her throat and initiated a conversation. "This is a real treat for me."

"What's a treat?" He looked up from mincing green onions.

"A man cooking for me. Are you sure I can't help?"

"No, everything's under control. Relax and enjoy."

She squirmed on the stool. "That's easier said than done. I can't believe I'm doing this."

"What can't you believe?"

"That I'm having a . . . sleep-over with a man I'm not married to."

Carter cracked up. The knife slipped, and a slice of green onion sailed off the cutting board and onto the floor. "A sleep-over! You make it sound like we're two kids planning to camp out in the backyard." Still laughing, he picked the onion off the floor and tossed it into the garbage disposal side of the double sink.

Face flaming, Jenny lowered her head. "Well, what would you call what we're doing? Labeling it an affair seems too tacky."

"You're embarrassed."

"A little." She glanced up to find him gazing solemnly at her. "I feel like my mother ought to walk in any minute now and box my ears for misbehaving." She'd meant for that to make him laugh. He didn't.

He frowned for a moment, then he laid the knife on the cutting board. "Don't be embarrassed, Jenny. We're adults, not kids."

"I know that, but . . ."

"But what?"

"I don't know how to act," she admitted. "I thought I could be casual and sophisticated about the whole thing." She sighed. "But I can no more pull off that kind of act than I can sprout wings and fly."

"You don't have to be anything but yourself."

"I was being myself and it turned you off." She regretted the words the moment they were out. "I'm sorry. Forget I said that."

He looked surprised. "I don't know what you're talking about."

"When we were kissing, I thought we were setting each other on fire." She felt a blush creep up her neck. "Then all of a sudden you acted like I had a disease or something. You couldn't get away from me fast enough. Did I come on too strong or something?"

His eyes looked turbulent, as though he were wrestling with the decision of whether to tell her the truth. Finally, he met her gaze squarely and said, "No, Jenny, you didn't come on too strong. It was me. I got . . ." He paused and ran his fingers through his hair. "God, this is hard." He drew in a deep breath and started over again. "I got scared."

She stared at him, speechless.

"That's right. I got scared." He braced his hands on the island, looking everywhere but at her. "Since my marriage ended, I've kept my relationships brief. No strings, no promises. I haven't allowed myself to focus on any one woman, because, frankly, I didn't want to care too deeply for a woman.

"I care about you, Jenny. Sometimes, I lie awake at night aching for you, for your touch, for your smile, your scent, your feel-good voice, for your laughter. I want you in my life."

She was so moved and filled with tenderness that she could barely speak. "Oh, Carter. Do you have any idea how that makes me feel to hear you say that? For me to know you care that much?" She almost told him she loved him, but a tightening of his mouth stopped her.

"I want you in my life," he repeated, looking grim. "We can be friends. We can be lovers. Just don't expect love and promises from me. I'm sorry, Jenny, but I don't believe I'm capable of giving more. Can you accept that?"

Shaken to the core, she couldn't answer for a long moment. Accept what he was willing to give, or walk away? She reached for her wine and quickly downed it. The choice narrowed to one, because she knew, no matter how much it might hurt in the end, she wasn't going to walk away.

She wasn't prepared to give up on the hope that he would come to realize he did love her. They had something rare and precious between them. Wasn't a relationship that held so much promise worth a little patience and, if need be, a little heartache?

Clinging to her hope, she lifted her chin and met his gaze. Determination filled her. She was unwilling to accept defeat without a fight. Lead with her heart, that's all she could honestly do.

"Okay, Carter," she said finally. "I'll try to accept what you feel you can give. No strings. No promises. We'll take it one day at a time."

Jenny was gone the next morning when he woke up. Carter felt a sharp, swift loss when he reached out and found the bed empty beside him. He sat up and focused on the chair where she'd laid her clothes and her canvas bag the night before. The chair was empty. He listened intently for a moment, hoping to hear the shower running in the next room, hoping some small sound would assure him she was still in the house.

Nothing broke the silence but the chirping of birds outside.

He lay back and explored the hollow feeling inside him. He'd spent a great evening laughing and making love with a woman who made him burn with desire, and now she was gone. That was the way a no-strings, no-promises relationship worked. Throughout the night they'd given each other warmth and passion and companionship. The sun was up, and it was over . . . for now.

Why should he feel so empty? He should be glad she had elected to play by his rules. He should be glad she wasn't there to snuggle her sweet little body against him. He should be grateful she hadn't made emotional demands he couldn't meet.

Why should he feel so damned lonely and empty?

Because she was gone.

Because she'd slipped out of his bed without waking him, without a kiss, without a word of good-bye.

ELEVEN

A week passed during which Jenny felt the strain of keeping her love for Carter hidden. Sometimes she wished she could knock some sense into him, shake him until he let go of the iron grip he kept on his emotions.

Right now, though, she wanted to shake him for a different reason. He and JoJo were having a personal battle of wills, and it was turning their roundtable discussion into a nightmare.

"JoJo, please stop kicking your chair," Carter said. "Can't you sit still for a minute?"

"No." Staring defiantly, she gave her chair another hard kick.

Seeing the storm brewing in both their eyes, Jenny quickly sought to defuse the situation. "JoJo, my little soldier, you're good at coming up with ideas. I appoint you our official Ways and Means Committee chairperson. How do you think we could earn the money to pay for our trip to Caro-Winds this summer?"

The child slammed her small fist down on the table. "I don't care about no damn Caro-Winds!"

Carter's face almost turned purple. "Young lady, that kind of language is not acceptable."

"You can't tell me what I can say or do. You're not the boss of me!"

Jenny quickly put her hand on Carter's knee, hoping to gain his attention and keep him from exploding. He whipped his head around to meet her gaze. She gave him a tiny pleading smile. He didn't appear happy about yielding the floor to her, but he did.

She looked at the sullen expression on JoJo's face. Something was wrong. "Why don't you care?" she asked calmly.

"I hate Caro-Winds." JoJo grabbed her copy of the agenda Carter had given the girls and ripped it in half. "My dad took me there last year for my birthday. Caro-Winds is stupid." She balled the torn paper in her hands and threw it across the table. "Birthdays are stupid. Stupid, stupid, stupid," she finished on a shout, then burst into tears.

Understanding came instantly to Jenny. Yesterday was JoJo's tenth birthday, and she guessed the child was upset because her father had disappointed her in some way. Her heart went out to the little girl. She sighed, thinking of the cake and party hats she had secretly stashed in the kitchen before the meeting, and she wondered if JoJo would find them a comfort or a poor substitute for the father's attention that she really wanted.

She got up and took the sobbing child into her arms. JoJo resisted for a second, then held on tight as she cried out her hurt and anger.

Finally she hiccuped, "H-he for-for-got my birth-day." She raised her head. "He didn't mean to, though." The fiercely protective note in her voice and the look on her face defied anyone to argue with that last vehement statement. Jenny knew that JoJo was her daddy's girl.

"I'm sure he didn't, sweetie," Jenny said, smoothing back the child's wayward blond locks. "I'm sure your father loves you very much."

"Yeah." JoJo wiped her nose with the back of her hand and pulled away to sit spine-stiff in her chair. "Dad got married last week. I guess he just had too many important things on his mind to think about me."

Carter felt like a heel. He'd been on the kid's case all morning. He hadn't once considered that there might be something behind her disruptive behavior besides plain orneriness.

"I know your father is going to be so upset when he realizes he missed your special day," Jenny said to JoJo.

Carter was damn upset with the man himself, and he didn't even know him. How could a father forget his own child's birthday? he wondered angrily. So what if the man just got married again. In his book, that was no excuse.

Something had to be done, he thought as he stared at JoJo. But what?

He glanced around the table at the other children as though their solemn faces might give him a clue. The caring and empathy in their eyes made him feel a burst of pride.

Surely there was something he could do to help JoJo, something that would show her he cared too. Something that would show her that he was sorry for being callous and impatient with her.

Suddenly, he thought of the birthday cake and party hats he'd seen Jenny hide in the kitchen before the meeting began. He automatically glanced at his watch. It wasn't snack time, and they weren't through with the business at hand.

Go with the flow.

As Jenny had told him more than once, one had to know when it was more important to throw schedules and timetables out the window and just go with the flow.

Lara was sitting next to him. He leaned down and whispered to her, "Your mom planned a surprise for JoJo. Will you help me get it ready?"

She beamed an approving smile. "Let's all go," she whispered back.

He nodded.

Between the two of them, they quietly spread the word to the others, then they all tiptoed into the kitchen.

A few minutes later, Carter came out bearing a cake lit with candles. The kids followed him, carrying the party hats, napkins, plates, cups, and drinks. He led them in singing "Happy Birthday" with more gusto than finesse.

JoJo stared openmouthed until the last word was sung. She sat so stiff and silent that for one terrible moment, Carter feared he had made a grave mistake. Then a tiny smile formed on her lips. The smile grew into a crooked grin.

"A party for me?" Her grin gave way to laughter.

Everybody laughed with her.

Carter set the cake down in front of her. "Make a wish, Miss Mouth," he said, hardly realizing he'd picked up on Jenny's habit of bestowing pet names on the girls. He tweaked JoJo's nose. "Make it a good one. It has to last a whole year, you know."

She smiled up at him, and he wanted to kick himself. He didn't deserve that grateful smile.

He watched her squeeze her eyes shut and bite her bottom lip as though wishing with every bit of strength in her wiry body. She blew out the candles, then clapped her hands and shouted, "All right, you morons! It's party time." It was so typically—and thankfully—JoJo that Carter didn't even wince at the earsplitting volume of her voice or that awful word "morons."

As the children gathered around her, all talking at once, Carter met Jenny's gaze over their heads. The glowing expression in her eyes, the smile on her face, assured him he'd done the right thing, and told him more eloquently than words that she was proud of him. He didn't quite recognize the warm sensation filling his heart, mind, and soul. It seemed sweet and painful at the same time.

He felt something was slipping away from him. This time he did recognize the feeling—the loosening of the tight rein he kept on his emotions. It scared him. He couldn't afford to give Jenny his heart. With the gift of love came the power to inflict pain. He reminded himself that all he could afford to give her was passion and friendship.

During the party, Jenny couldn't keep her eyes off Carter. She was on automatic pilot, talking, laughing, and partying with the children. Inside, she was bursting with love, and she marveled that it didn't explode out of her and light up the room.

There was so much kindness in Carter, she thought as she listened to him telling JoJo and the other kids a funny story about one of his brother's birthdays. His brother's birthday was the day after Christmas, and their mother, preoccupied with holiday preparations, had forgotten about his cake, so she had improvised with a cinnamon bun and a candle.

There was more than desire when he touched her, she knew. There was a deep sense of caring. At times she was certain he was on the edge of giving her the love she needed so badly.

When the party broke up and the kids were leaving, she followed Carter into the tiny kitchen at the back of the activity room. Her heart was bursting with love for him and with pride for the compassion he'd shown a child suffering the pain of rejection.

"Hi." He gave her a smile, though he looked a bit drained. "That was a close call, wasn't it? I can't believe I didn't pick up on the clues that something was bothering JoJo."

She put her arms around his waist. "She went home happy."

"She did, didn't she?" he said, brightening.

Jenny rested her head against his chest. When he bent down to kiss the top of her head and his hand stroked her hair, she closed her eyes and surrendered all the love fighting to be free inside her.

"Oh, Carter, I love you."

Caught up in the depth of her own emotions, it took her a moment to feel the stiffening of his body. Her mind cleared, and she noticed the tensing of his hands on her shoulders. She kept her eyes shut, knowing that the words had been spoken and she could not take them back.

"I'm sorry." She stepped away from him and looked up. She couldn't tell what he was thinking. His expression was shuttered, but she could feel him distancing himself. "I'm not sorry that I love you. I'm sorry you don't want me to feel that way."

He leaned back against the cabinet and folded his arms. More distancing, she thought sadly. "You don't mean that. You're just overreacting to an emotional day."

Her voice was not quite steady when she spoke. "You don't believe I love you?"

"People think they're in love all the time. They say things they don't mean and make promises they can't keep. Let's not mess up what we have with pretty but meaningless words."

She could only stand and stare at him.

To Carter, she looked as vulnerable and hurt as a child. He turned away and picked up a pile of unused paper plates. His hands were shaking as he stuffed the plates into a cardboard box.

"I said I loved you." Her voice rose. "I don't lie. I'm not demanding that you love me back. Dammit, look at me!"

It was the first time he'd ever heard her swear. Surprised, he turned on his heel. Their eyes locked; hers were intractable. He saw tears rise, and his throat tightened. He'd never seen her cry before, and her tears tugged at his heart. He felt too damn much for her.

She might think she loved him, but he knew it wouldn't take her long to realize differently. It was up to him to be sensible, to keep his head, to make sure they didn't lose what they had together.

After a moment he said, "Don't hate me for not being the sentimental, emotional man you want me to be."

"I could never hate you." She drew in a breath, then let it out slowly.

He felt a quickening of fear at the defeat he saw in her face. He was losing her. "Do you want to get married?" he asked out of desperation. "Is that it? We can make this thing legal, if it's important to you. We care about each other. It might work."

She opened her mouth, then shut it before she attempted to speak. "I appreciate the offer, but I have to pass." She grabbed her purse from the counter and turned to leave.

"What do you want from me?" he called out angrily.

She turned around and looked at him, dark eyes flashing. "I know what I don't want. I had a husband who was incapable of loving me, and I know I don't want another one."

"Jenny, I'm sorry. I wish—"

She held up her hand to silence him. "It's all right, Carter. You don't have to let me down gently. I'm not going to make a big emotional scene." Her voice cracked, and she wheeled away, back stiff. "I've been run over by this train before."

Gazing at her, he half wanted to take the few steps separating them and slip his arms around her. But he knew he'd lose it if he touched her. One touch and something would shatter like thin crystal inside him.

The silence stretched, pulling so tight that the air in the room all but vibrated with it. Carter wondered desperately how the situation had gotten so out of hand so quickly.

"What the hell do you want me to say, Jenny?" he asked more savagely than he'd meant to.

"You could say that you love me."

He raked his hand through his hair. "I want you in my life. Isn't that enough?"

Her eyes were still dark with anger and some other fierce emotion that Carter didn't even want to think about. She held his gaze for one painful moment, then said quietly, "No, it isn't enough."

"Are you saying it's over between us? You don't want to see me anymore?"

She dropped her gaze. When she spoke, her voice was flat, as though all emotion had drained from her. "Yes, I guess I am. I'll still take care of Tiffany after school, if you want me to. But when you come to pick her up, don't linger."

"I'll call you."

"Please don't." She glanced at him, and he saw the pain in her eyes.

"Jenny, I'm sorry."

She shook her head. "I don't want you to be sorry. I want you to search your mind and your heart. If you honestly feel you can never love me, then please just do as I ask and stay away from me. It will hurt, but I'll survive." She paused, then added softly, "Nothing hurts forever."

Carter watched her leave the room. For a long time, he simply stood there. Even when he heard Tiffany call him, he just stood there.

And he felt sickeningly empty.

❖———————❖

"I didn't think it would hurt so bad," Jenny said to her sister two weeks later. She'd stopped in Maureen's classroom after school for a quick visit.

Maureen put her arm around her. "Carter Dalton ought to be strung up by his thumbs. From the way he looked at you at my dinner party, I was so sure he was falling in love with you. I'm sorry I ever gave that bum your phone number and address. This is all my fault."

"He isn't a bum." She wiped tears from her cheeks with the back of her hand. "He's wonderful. It's not your fault. It's not his fault either, if he can't love me."

Maureen drew back far enough to study Jenny's face. "This is the real thing, isn't it?"

"Oh yeah."

"Then don't give up on him. Fight for what you want."

"I'm trying." Jenny sighed and brushed her hands over her face. "Lord, I'm a mess."

"Look, why don't you go home and get some rest. I'll take the kids to the Y for you. They can get someone else to teach your class."

"Thanks, Mo, but I need to keep busy." She tried to smile. "Thanks for letting me cry on your shoulder."

"Hey, no problem." Maureen hugged her. "That's what big sisters are for."

Jenny pulled herself together as she walked down the hall to the school library where Lara and Tiffany were searching for reference materials for class projects. Whenever she was with them she tried to be bright and happy, but they had picked up on the strain between their parents. Lara missed Carter almost as much as Jenny did. Tiffany clung to her every evening when her father came to take her home. Even the Sunshine Girls knew something wasn't quite right, and they responded to the tension by being unusually quiet and subdued.

Jenny didn't know what to say to any of them to make them understand what was going on. She just kept on playing Pollyanna, living on the hope that Carter would come to realize he loved her as much as she loved him.

Somehow she managed to keep a smile on her face and a steady stream of conversation going with the girls as she settled them in the minivan. A block from the YMCA, the vehicles in front of her came to a sudden stop. Jenny reacted quickly, stomping her foot down hard on the brake. The van jerked to a halt mere inches from kissing the bumper of a red Mustang.

She breathed a sigh of relief. Then she silently said a few unkind things about the nut in front of the Mustang who had decided to stop and make a left-hand turn without signaling.

Suddenly, she heard the shriek of rubber on asphalt. Her gaze flew to the rearview mirror. A pickup truck was hurtling toward her.

"Girls, hang on!" she screamed, barely having time to brace herself before the truck smashed into their rear bumper.

The impact was bone jarring. It threw her against her shoulder harness and it snapped tight, but not tight enough. The breath was knocked out of her as her forehead and chin struck the steering wheel. The van pitched forward and rammed into the Mustang.

The second impact was almost as hard.

Lara and Tiffany wailed in fear.

Half-blinded and dazed by shock and pain, Jenny slumped down in the seat. Shivering uncontrollably, she fought off a wave of nausea.

TWELVE

Carter gave up all pretense of working. He couldn't concentrate. Burlington Industries would just have to wait another day for his report on how they could save time, energy, and money.

He missed Jenny so badly that it was a constant ache in his gut. He longed for her warmth, her beautiful smile, the way her eyes sparkled with laughter, and the tenderness of her touch.

Everything was different now. When he went to her house after work, the children no longer latched on to him as he came through the door, demanding his attention and both talking excitedly about the day's events. It made him feel as though he'd lost a part of his family.

He even missed that rude parrot, the drooling hound from hell, the cats, and the puppy that constantly managed to get underfoot and trip him up.

He got up from his desk and went to stare out

his office window. It was a beautiful day. The grass was as green as the Emerald Isle, and everywhere he looked there was a profusion of flowers and shrubs in bloom. Above it all was a sky so clear and bright, it hurt to stare up at it too long. But he was in no mood to appreciate the wonders of nature.

For two weeks he'd shied away from searching his heart and mind. Instead, he'd tried to convince himself to let her go. She was better off without him, he told himself. But he wasn't better off without her. She was the best thing that had ever happened to him. She added richness to his life.

"I'm in love with Jenny." The words came with a slow shattering of the defenses he'd lived with since his ex-wife had told him she didn't love him anymore. But was he emotionally strong enough to give Jenny everything she needed?

God, he hoped so.

Carter rubbed his hands over his face. He'd made such a mess of things. He hoped it wasn't too late to make amends.

Returning to his desk, he stuffed the Burlington report in a file folder. As he checked the contents of his briefcase, he heard the phone ring in the outer chamber. A moment later, his secretary buzzed him. He picked up the phone and without preamble said, "I'm not available, Anne. Take a message. I'm leaving for the day."

"B-but, Carter," his secretary stammered. "Someone from Cone Memorial Hospital called and said that your daughter is in the emergency room. She was involved in a car accident."

He stopped breathing. Clutching the phone receiver so tight, his knuckles turned white, Carter fought to control a scream of rage and fear. He drew a painful breath. "Are they still on the line?"

"Oh, no. They said that Tiffany isn't hurt and neither is Mrs. Johnson's daughter. They're just shaken up a bit. It's Mrs. Johnson they're concerned about."

Jenny was hurt.

His skin turned ice-cold. Carter dropped the phone. He grabbed his car keys and bolted out of the room, leaving his suit jacket and briefcase behind.

Carter entered the hospital emergency room with only one thought running through his head. Jenny had to be okay, so they could make things right between them.

In the waiting room, he saw Tiffany and Lara sitting with a policewoman. Relieved that they looked uninjured, yet still scared to death for the woman he loved, he rushed over to them and scooped the children up into his arms. He couldn't stop kissing and hugging them both.

"We got hit," Lara said, when he finally set both girls down again. "By a pickup truck. The kind with those great big wheels."

"Jenny hit her head." Tears welled up in Tiffany's eyes, and she looked scared.

"It wasn't my mom's fault. Honest, it wasn't. Please don't be mad at her anymore." Lara dropped her face into her hands.

Both children started crying.

Carter felt like joining them. "Everything's going to be all right," he said, putting an arm around each of them. "Lara, I'm not mad at your mother. I love her."

"Are you gonna marry her?" She raised her head and looked at him with hope shining in her brown eyes.

"If she'll have me. Would that be okay with you girls?"

Lara and Tiffany exchanged glances. "We can really be sisters," they said at the same time.

That was all the approval Carter needed. He spoke briefly with the police officer who explained what had happened, then went to look for Jenny.

The tears she thought she didn't have left in her sprang to Jenny's eyes the moment Carter walked into the tiny examining cubicle. Emotion crawled through her like a living thing.

"Oh, Carter! I'm so sorry." She struggled to sit up. "Did you see the girls? Are they all right? I—" A sob rose up in her throat, and she couldn't go on.

"Hush. Don't upset yourself." He took her in

his arms and held her as though he might never let her go again. "The kids are fine. I talked to the doctor. He said they might be a little sore from being jerked around, but that will pass in a day or two. You're the one we're worried about. He said you have a concussion and some nasty bruises. You're not going to feel too swift for a while. Thank God you were wearing your seat belt. You could have been thrown through the windshield."

The tenderness in his voice made her cry harder. His arms tightened around her gently, and he buried his face in her hair. "Jenny," he said in an agonized whisper, "I never meant to hurt you."

"I know." She stopped crying and met his gaze. "It doesn't matter now."

"It does matter." He took her hands and brought them to his lips. "I know the timing isn't perfect, sweetheart, but I have something to tell you."

She yanked her hands away and covered her face. "No, don't. Not now." She'd had more than she could take. She didn't want to hear him say it was all over between them.

"Please," he said in a low, urgent voice. "I *need* you to listen to me."

It took every bit of courage she possessed to drop her hands into her lap and look at him. "All right, Carter, I'm listening."

"This should be so simple." He caressed her cheek with trembling fingers. "I ought to go down on one knee, but then you'd probably fall off the examining table trying to see me." He laughed shakily and took a deep breath. "I love you. There, I said it, and I haven't been struck by lightning. And you . . . you still love me, don't you?"

For a moment, she could only stare at him. "You love me?"

He nodded. "With all my heart. I love Lara too. I know part of it is because she's your daughter, but there's more. There's something sweet and loving about her that makes me want to take care of her like she's mine. When you and I and the girls are together, it feels like we've always been a family. The feeling fills empty places in me that I didn't even know I had."

Jenny bit her lip to stop the spill of more tears. She could hardly believe what she was hearing. Certain the deep, abiding love she felt for him must be shining out of her, she lifted her trembling hand to his face. "Carter, you have perfect timing. There's nothing on earth I've wanted more than to hear you say you love me."

He gazed down at her, his eyes brimming with emotion. "I love you. Will you marry me and give me a lifetime to prove it?"

She laughed through her tears. "Yes, and that's a promise you can count on, champ."

He lowered his head to kiss her, and she sank into the sweetness of him. His hands were warm and strong as he caressed her back, and she felt a shiver of anticipation wind through her.

"Mrs. Jennifer Kathleen Dalton-to-be," he

whispered against her lips, "tomorrow we're going to visit a jeweler, get a marriage license, and find a minister."

She laughed. "Once you make up your mind to do something, you don't waste any time, do you?"

"Never put off what you can do today. I want you in my life and in my home as soon as possible."

"Your home? I don't know if I can live at your house," she teased. "It's too neat."

He gave a long, lazy laugh, cradling her against him. "It won't be, after you move in with your stuff and your zoo. You can hang Aunt Charlotte's paintings on the walls and mess the place up to your heart's content. And if that doesn't make you feel at home, we'll invite the Sunshine Girls over and let them have at it."

Jenny looked up at him, her face radiant with love. "Take me home, Carter."

He swung her up into his arms and into the lifetime of love-filled adventures that awaited them.

THE EDITOR'S CORNER

The end of summer means back to school and cooler weather, but here at LOVESWEPT temperatures are rising with four sensational romances to celebrate the beginning of autumn. You'll thrill to the sexiest heroes and cheer for the most spirited heroines as they discover the power of passion. They're sure to heat up your reading hours with their wonderful, sensuous tales.

Leading our lineup is the marvelously talented Debra Dixon with **MOUNTAIN MYSTIC**, LOVESWEPT # 706. Joshua Logan has always been able to read anyone's emotions, but he can't figure Victoria Bennett out—maybe because his longing for the beautiful midwife is so unexpected! He'd come home to the mountains seeking refuge from a world that demanded more than he could give; why now did he have to meet a woman who awakened his need to touch and be touched? Debra weaves a moving story of trust and healing that you won't forget.

Donna Kauffman invites you to meet a **BOUNTY HUNTER,** LOVESWEPT # 707. Kane Hawthorne was hired to locate a runaway wife, but when he finds Elizabeth Lawson, he knows he has to claim her as his own! A desperate woman who dares trust no one, she tries to keep him from making her enemies his, but Kane insists on fighting her demons. And she has no choice but to cherish her savage hero until his own ghosts are silenced. With this electrifying romance Donna proves that nobody does it better when it comes to writing about a dangerous and sexy man.

Cindy Gerard's newest book will keep you awake long **INTO THE NIGHT,** LOVESWEPT # 708. It began as a clever gimmick to promote a radio show for lovers, but the spirited sparring between Jessie Fox and Tony Falcone is so believable, listeners demand to know more of their steamy romance! Jessie vows it is impossible for this gorgeous younger man to want her with the fire she sees burning in his eyes —until the brash Falcon sets a seductive trap his Fox can't escape. Cindy's irresistible blend of humor and playful passion creates a memorable couple you will cherish.

The ever popular Peggy Webb has written her most sensual and heartbreaking novel yet with **ONLY HIS TOUCH,** LOVESWEPT # 709. For years Kathleen Shaw's body had danced to the music of Hunter La Farge's mouth and hands, but when the beautiful ballerina loses everything she'd lived for in a shocking accident, the untamed adventurer is the last man she wants to face. Twice before he'd lost the woman who shared his soul, but now the fierce panther who had claimed her for all time must set her free to recapture her dream. This is Peggy at her best—keep a box of tissues handy!

I'd like to take this opportunity to share with you some exciting news. I have been promoted to Deputy Publisher here at Bantam and will consequently be managing all aspects of the Bantam adult hardcover, trade, and mass-market paperback publishing program. I will continue to oversee women's fiction, but most of the hands-on work will be handled by Senior Editor Beth de Guzman, Assistant Editor Shauna Summers, and Administrative Editor Gina Iemolo. Of course, none of this changes our team's continuing goal to bring you the best in contemporary romantic fiction written by the most talented and loved authors in the genre.

Happy reading!

With warmest wishes,

Nita Taublib

Nita Taublib
Deputy Publisher

P.S. Don't miss the exciting women's novels from Bantam that are coming your way in September—**ADAM'S FALL** is the paperback reprint of the classic romantic novel from *New York Times* bestselling author Sandra Brown; **THE LAST BACHELOR,** from nationally bestselling author Betina Krahn, is a spectacularly entertaining battle of the sexes set in Victorian England; **PRINCE OF WOLVES,** by Susan Krinard, is a spellbinding new romance of mystery, magic, and forbidden passion in the tradition of Linda Lael Miller; and **WHISPERED LIES** is the latest novel from Christy Cohen, about two intimate strangers divided by dangerous secrets, broken vows, and misplaced passions. We'll be giving you a sneak peek at these terrific books in next month's LOVE-SWEPTs. And immediately following this page look for a preview of the exciting romances from Bantam that are *available now!*

Don't miss these electrifying books by
your favorite Bantam authors

On sale in July:

MIDNIGHT WARRIOR

by Iris Johansen

BLUE MOON

by Luanne Rice

VELVET

by Jane Feather

WITCH DANCE

by Peggy Webb

Winner of *Romantic Times*'s
Career Achievement Award

Iris Johansen

THE *NEW YORK TIMES* BESTSELLING
AUTHOR OF
THE BELOVED SCOUNDREL

MIDNIGHT WARRIOR

*From the author who has been lauded as "the Mistress of
Romantic Fantasy" comes a passionate new tale of danger,
adventure, and romance that sweeps from a Saxon strong-
hold to a lovers' bower in the cool, jade-green forests of
Wales. . . .*

Brynn hesitated for a moment and then said reluctantly, "This is a bad place. Can't you feel it?"

"Feel what?"

"If you cannot feel it, I can't explain. I just want to
be gone from here." She paused and then whispered,
"Please."

He looked at her in surprise. "This must mean a
good deal to you. You're more given to commands
than pleas."

She didn't answer.

"What if I give you what you wish?" He lowered his voice to silky softness. "Will you give me a gift in turn?"

"I've given you a gift. Your friend Malik is alive. Isn't that enough for you?"

"It should be."

"But it isn't?"

"Malik will tell you I don't know the meaning of enough. The prize just over the horizon is always the sweetest."

"So you reach out and take it," she said flatly.

"Or barter for it. I prefer the latter. It suits my merchant's soul. I suppose Malik has told you that I'm more trader than knight?"

"No, he said you were the son of a king and capable of being anything you wanted to be."

"Which obviously did not impress you."

"Why should it? It does not matter their station, men are all the same."

He smiled. "Certainly in some aspects. You didn't answer. Will you barter with me?"

"I have nothing with which to barter."

"You're a woman. A woman always has great bartering power."

She straightened her shoulders and turned to look directly at him. "You mean you wish me to be your whore."

His lips tightened. "Your words lack a certain delicacy."

"They do not lack truth." She looked down into the pot. "You wish me to part my limbs and let you rut like a beast of the forest. I wonder you even seek to bargain. You think me your slave. Isn't a slave to be used?"

"Yes," he said curtly. "A slave is to work and give

pleasure. And you're right, I don't have to bargain with you. I can do what I wish."

"I'm glad that is clear." She stirred faster, harder. "Shall we go into the tent now? Or perhaps you wish to take me in front of all your soldiers? I'd be grateful if you'd have the kindness to let me finish preparing this salve that is making your friend well and healthy. But if I seem unreasonable, you must only tell me and I will—"

"Be silent!" His teeth clenched, he added, "I've never met a woman with such a—"

"I'm only being humble and obliging. Isn't that what you want of me?"

"I want—" He stopped and then said thickly, "I'm not certain what I want . . . yet. When I do, I'll be sure you're made fully aware of it."

"Rice has an elegant style, a sharp eye and a real warmth. In her hands families—and their values—seem worth cherishing."
—*San Francisco Chronicle*

BLUE MOON

BY

Luanne Rice

BLUE MOON is a moving novel of a family that discovers the everyday magic of life and the extraordinary power of love. The New York Times *has already praised it as* "*a rare combination of realism and romance.*" Entertainment Weekly *has simply called it* "*brilliant,*" *and* People *has raved that it is* "*eloquent . . . a moving and complete tale of the complicated phenomenon we call family.*"

Here is a look at this powerful novel. . . .

After two weeks at sea, Billy Medieros was heading home. He usually loved this part of the trip, when the hold was full of fish and his crew was happy because they knew their share of the catch would be high, and they'd all sleep in their own beds that night. He drove the *Norboca*—the best boat in his father-in-law's fleet —around Minturn Ledge, and Mount Hope came into view.

Billy stood at the wheel. The tide had been against

him, and he knew he had missed Cass. She would have left work by now, was probably already home cooking supper. He could picture her at the stove, stirring something steamy, her summer dress sticking damply to her breasts and hips. His wife had the body of a young sexpot. Other guys at sea would pray to Miss July, but Billy would look at pictures of Cass, her coppery curls falling across her face, her blue eyes sexy and mysterious, delicate fingers cupping her full breasts, offering them to the camera. She had given him a Minolta for his last birthday, but for his real present she had posed nude.

Lately, to Billy, Cass had seemed more real in his bunk at sea than she was at home. In person, Cass looked the same, she smelled the same, but she seemed absent, somehow. Raising Josie changed her every day, and Billy resisted the transformation. He missed his wife.

He was nearly home. His eyes roved the church spires, the wooden piers clawing the harbor, American flags flapping from the yacht club and every hotel roof, white yachts rocking on the waves, two trawlers heading out. He waved to the skippers, both of whom he had fished with before. Manuel Vega waved back, a beer in his hand.

Billy couldn't stand skippers who drank onboard. It set a bad example for the crew. You had to stay keen every second. Billy had seen terrible things happen to fishermen who weren't paying attention—fingers lost to a winch handle, a skull split open by a boom. On Billy's first trip out with his father-in-law, Jimmy Keating, a crewmate with both hands busy setting nets had bitten down on a skinny line to hold it in place, and a gust of wind had yanked out six of his top teeth.

Stupid. Billy had no patience for stupid crew

members, and dulling your senses with alcohol, at sea on a fifty-foot boat, was stupid.

"Docking!" Billy yelled, and four guys ran up from below. John Barnard, Billy's first mate for this trip, stood with Billy at the bridge. They had gone to high school together; they'd fished as a team hundreds of times. They never confided in each other, but they had an easygoing way of passing time for long stretches.

Strange, maybe, considering that John Barnard was the only man Billy had ever felt jealous of. Cass liked him too much.

Not that anything had ever happened. But Billy knew she'd get that look in her eyes whenever she was going to see John. Before Christmas parties, Holy Ghost Society Dances, even goddamn PTA meetings. Cass was a flirt, for sure; it only made Billy that much prouder she belonged to him.

Cass and John had dated a couple of times after high school, when Cass had wanted to marry Billy and Billy had been too dumb to ask. Billy, delivering scallops to Lobsterville one night, had met Cass's mother in the kitchen.

"I want to show you something," Mary Keating said. She began leading Billy into the dining room.

"I can't go in there," Billy said, sniffing his sleeve. His rubber boots tracked fragments of scallop shells.

"You'd better, if you don't want to lose her," Mary said. Five-two in her red high heels, Mary Keating had a husky smoker's voice and the drive of a Detroit diesel. Standing in the kitchen doorway, blocking waiters, she pointed across the dining room. There, at a table for two, framed by a picture window overlooking a red sun setting over Mount Hope harbor, were Cass and John having dinner together.

Bonnie and Nora, in their waitress uniforms, hovered nearby.

John was tall, with sandy-brown hair and a movie-hero profile, and the way he and Cass were leaning across the table, smiling into each other's eyes, made Billy want to vault across the bar and smash John's face into his plate. He left without a word, but the incident brought Billy to his senses; two months later, he and Cass were married.

Billy pulled back on the throttle as they passed the No Wake buoy.

"Almost there," John said.

"Can I grab a ride with you?" Billy asked. The Barnards, like most fishing families, lived in Alewives Park.

"Sure," John said. "No problem."

The deck hands checked the dock lines, then stood along the port rail, waiting to jump ashore. Billy threw the engine into reverse, then eased the boat ahead. She bumped hard once, hard again, and then settled into a gentle sway.

In the bestselling tradition of
Amanda Quick, a spectacular new
historical romance from the nationally
bestselling

Jane Feather

"An author to treasure."
—*Romantic Times*

VELVET

*Clad in black velvet and posing as a widowed French com-
tesse, Gabrielle de Beaucaire had returned to England for
one purpose only—to ruin the man responsible for her
young lover's death. But convincing the forbidding Nathaniel Praed, England's greatest spymaster, that she
would make the perfect agent for his secret service would
not be easy. And even after Gabrielle had lured the devastatingly attractive lord to her bed, she would have to con-
tend with his distrust—and with the unexpected hunger
that his merest touch aroused. . . .*

It was a bright clear night, the air crisp, the stars
sharp in the limitless black sky. He flung open the
window, leaning his elbows on the sill, looking out
over the expanse of smooth lawn where frost glittered

under the starlight. It would be a beautiful morning for the hunt.

He climbed back into bed and blew out his candle.

He heard the rustling of the woodbine almost immediately. His hand slipped beneath his pillow to his constant companion, the small silver-mounted pistol. He lay very still, every muscle held in waiting, his ears straining into the darkness. The small scratching, rustling sounds continued, drawing closer to the open window. Someone was climbing the thick ancient creeper clinging to the mellow brick walls of the Jacobean manor house.

His hand closed more firmly over the pistol and he hitched himself up on one elbow, his eyes on the square of the window, waiting.

Hands competently gripped the edge of the windowsill, followed by a dark head. The nocturnal visitor swung a leg over the sill and hitched himself upright, straddling the sill.

"Since you've only just snuffed your candle, I'm sure you're still awake," Gabrielle de Beaucaire said into the dark, still room. "And I'm sure you have a pistol, so please don't shoot, it's only me."

Nathaniel was rarely taken by surprise and was a master at concealing it on those rare occasions. On this occasion, however, his training deserted him.

"*Only!*" he exclaimed. "What the hell are you doing?"

"Guess," his visitor challenged cheerfully from her perch.

"You'll have to forgive me, but I don't find guessing games amusing," he declared in clipped accents. He sat up, his pistol still in his hand, and stared at the dark shape outlined against the moonlight. That aura of trouble surrounding Gabrielle de Beaucaire had not been a figment of his imagination.

"Perhaps I should be flattered," he said icily. "Am I to assume unbridled lust lies behind the honor of this visit, madam?" His eyes narrowed.

Disconcertingly, the woman appeared to be impervious to irony. She laughed. A warm, merry sound that Nathaniel found as incongruous in the circumstances as it was disturbingly attractive.

"Not at his point, Lord Praed; but there's no saying what the future might hold." It was a mischievous and outrageous statement that rendered him temporarily speechless.

She took something out of the pocket of her britches and held it on the palm of her hand. "I'm here to present my credentials."

She swung off the windowsill and approached the bed, a sinuous figure in her black britches and glimmering white shirt.

He leaned sideways, struck flint on tinder, and re-lit the bedside candle. The dark red hair glowed in the light as she extended her hand, palm upward, toward him and he saw what she held.

It was a small scrap of black velvet cut with a ragged edge.

"Well, well." The evening's puzzles were finally solved. Lord Praed opened a drawer in the bedside table and took out a piece of tissue paper. Unfolding it, he revealed the twin of the scrap of material.

"I should have guessed," he said pensively. "Only a woman would have come up with such a fanciful idea." He took the velvet from her extended palm and fitted the ragged edge to the other piece, making a whole square. "So you're Simon's surprise. No wonder he was so secretive. But what makes you think I would ever employ a woman?"

WITCH DANCE

BY

Peggy Webb

"Ms. Webb has an inventive mind brimming with originality that makes all of her books special reading."—*Romantic Times*

An exquisite woman of ivory and jade, she'd come to Witch Dance, Oklahoma, to bring modern medicine to the native Chickasaw people. But when Dr. Kate Malone saw the magnificent Indian rising from the river, naked as sin and twice as tempting, every thought of duty was lost, drowned in a primitive wave of longing that made her tremble with desire. . . .

He was more man than she'd ever seen. And every gorgeous inch of him was within touching distance.

For all he seemed to care, he could have been bending over her in a Brooks Brothers suit.

"What impulse sent you into the river?" He squatted beside her with both hands on her shoulders, and she'd never felt skin as hot in her life.

" I thought you were drowning."

His laughter was deep and melodious, and as sensual as exotic music played in some dark corner of a dimly lit café where lovers embraced.

"I am Chickasaw," he said, as if that explained everything.

"Well, I'm human and I made a mistake." She pushed her wet hair away from her face. "Why can't you just admit you made a mistake, staying under the water so long I thought you were going to drown?"

"You were watching me?"

"No . . . yes . . ." His legs were powerful, heavily muscled, bent in such a way that the best parts of him were hidden. He leaned closer, intent on answers. How did he expect her to think straight with his leg touching hers like that? "Not deliberately," she said. "I was on a picnic. How did I know you'd be cavorting about in the river without any clothes on?"

He searched her face with eyes deep and black. Then he touched her cheeks, his strong hands exquisitely gentle.

"I'm sorry I ruined your picnic." Ever so tenderly his hands roamed over her face. Breathless, she sat beside the river, his willing captive. "You've scratched your face . . . here . . . and here."

Until that moment she hadn't known that every nerve in the body could tremble. Now she could attest to it as a medical fact.

". . . and your legs." He gave her legs the same tender attention he'd given her face. She would have sold her soul to feel his hands on her forever. "I have remedies for your injuries."

Oh, God. Would he kiss them and make them well? She almost said it.

"I can fix them . . ." How? She could barely breathe. "I'm a doctor."

"You came to Tribal Lands to practice medicine?"

"You doubt my word?"

"No. Your commitment."

"Is it because I'm white that you think I'm not committed, or because I'm female?"

"Neither, *Wictonaye*." In one fluid movement he stood before her, smiling.

And in that moment her world changed. Colors

and light receded, faded, until there was nothing except the bold Chickasaw with his glowing, polished skin and his seductive voice that obliterated every thought, every need except the most basic . . . to die of love. Sitting on the hard ground, looking up at her nameless captor, she wanted to die in the throes of passion.

She stood on shaky, uncertain legs. Clenching her fists by her side, she faced him.

"If you're going to call me names, use English, please."

"*Wictonaye* . . . wildcat."

"I've been called worse." Would God forgive her if she left right now? Would He give her the healing touch and allow her to save lives if she forgot about her lust and focused on her mission?

She spun around, then felt his hand on her arm.

"I've been rude. It's not my way."

"Nor mine." She grinned. "Except sometimes."

"You tried to save my life, and I don't know your name."

"Kate Malone."

"Thank you for saving my life, Kate Malone." His eyes sparkled with wicked glee. She'd never known a man of such boldness . . . nor such appeal. "I'm Eagle Mingo."

"Next time you decide to play in the river, Eagle Mingo, be more careful. I might not be around to rescue you."

She marched toward the bluff, thinking it was a good exit, until he appeared beside her, still naked as sin and twice as tempting.

"You forgot your shoe." He held out one of her moccasins.

"Thanks." Lord, did he expect her to bend down

and put it on with him standing there like that? She hobbled along, half shoeless.

"And your picnic basket." He scooped it off the ground and handed it to her. Then, damned if he didn't bow like some courtly knight in shining armor.

If she ever got home, she'd have to take an aspirin and go to bed. Doctor's orders.

"Good-bye. Enjoy your"—her eyes raked him from head to toe, and she could feel her whole body getting hot—"swim."

She didn't know how she got up the bluff, but she didn't draw a good breath until she was safely at the top. He was still standing down there, looking up. She could feel his eyes on her.

Lest he think she was a total coward, she put on her other shoe, then turned and casually waved at him. At least she hoped it was casual.

Dammit all, he waved back. Facing full front. She might never recover.

And don't miss these incredible
romances from Bantam Books, on sale
in August:

THE LAST
BACHELOR
by the nationally bestselling author

Betina Krahn

"One of the genre's most creative writers."
—*Romantic Times*

PRINCE OF
WOLVES
by the sensational

Susan Krinard

A romance of mystery, magic, and
forbidden passion

WHISPERED LIES
by the highly acclaimed

Christy Cohen
A novel of dangerous desires and seductive
secrets

OFFICIAL RULES

To enter the sweepstakes below carefully follow all instructions found elsewhere in this offer.

The **Winners Classic** will award prizes with the following approximate maximum values: 1 Grand Prize: $26,500 (or $25,000 cash alternate); 1 First Prize: $3,000; 5 Second Prizes: $400 each; 35 Third Prizes: $100 each; 1,000 Fourth Prizes: $7.50 each. Total maximum retail value of Winners Classic Sweepstakes is $42,500. Some presentations of this sweepstakes may contain individual entry numbers corresponding to one or more of the aforementioned prize levels. To determine the Winners, individual entry numbers will first be compared with the winning numbers preselected by computer. For winning numbers not returned, prizes will be awarded in random drawings from among all eligible entries received. Prize choices may be offered at various levels. If a winner chooses an automobile prize, all license and registration fees, taxes, destination charges and, other expenses not offered herein are the responsibility of the winner. If a winner chooses a trip, travel must be complete within one year from the time the prize is awarded. Minors must be accompanied by an adult. Travel companion(s) must also sign release of liability. Trips are subject to space and departure availability. Certain black-out dates may apply.

The following applies to the sweepstakes named above:

No purchase necessary. You can also enter the sweepstakes by sending your name and address to: P.O. Box 508, Gibbstown, N.J. 08027. Mail each entry separately. Sweepstakes begins 6/1/93. Entries must be received by 12/30/94. Not responsible for lost, late, damaged, misdirected, illegible or postage due mail. Mechanically reproduced entries are not eligible. All entries become property of the sponsor and will not be returned.

Prize Selection/Validations: Selection of winners will be conducted no later than 5:00 PM on January 28, 1995, by an independent judging organization whose decisions are final. Random drawings will be held at 1211 Avenue of the Americas, New York, N.Y. 10036. Entrants need not be present to win. Odds of winning are determined by total number of entries received. Circulation of this sweepstakes is estimated not to exceed 200 million. All prizes are guaranteed to be awarded and delivered to winners. Winners will be notified by mail and may be required to complete an affidavit of eligibility and release of liability which must be returned within 14 days of date on notification or alternate winners will be selected in a random drawing. Any prize notification letter or any prize returned to a participating sponsor, Bantam Doubleday Dell Publishing Group, Inc., its participating divisions or subsidiaries, or the independent judging organization as undeliverable will be awarded to an alternate winner. Prizes are not transferable. No substitution for prizes except as offered or as may be necessary due to unavailability, in which case a prize of equal or greater value will be awarded. Prizes will be awarded approximately 90 days after the drawing. All taxes are the sole responsibility of the winners. Entry constitutes permission (except where prohibited by law) to use winners' names, hometowns, and likenesses for publicity purposes without further or other compensation. Prizes won by minors will be awarded in the name of parent or legal guardian.

Participation: Sweepstakes open to residents of the United States and Canada, except for the province of Quebec. Sweepstakes sponsored by Bantam Doubleday Dell Publishing Group, Inc., (BDD), 1540 Broadway, New York, NY 10036. Versions of this sweepstakes with different graphics and prize choices will be offered in conjunction with various solicitations or promotions by different subsidiaries and divisions of BDD. Where applicable, winners will have their choice of any prize offered at level won. Employees of BDD, its divisions, subsidiaries, advertising agencies, independent judging organization, and their immediate family members are not eligible.

Canadian residents, in order to win, must first correctly answer a time limited arithmetical skill testing question. Void in Puerto Rico, Quebec and wherever prohibited or restricted by law. Subject to all federal, state, local and provincial laws and regulations. For a list of major prize winners (available after 1/29/95): send a self-addressed, stamped envelope entirely separate from your entry to: Sweepstakes Winners, P.O. Box 517, Gibbstown, NJ 08027. Requests must be received by 12/30/94. DO NOT SEND ANY OTHER CORRESPONDENCE TO THIS P.O. BOX.